STEPPING ON THE CRACKS

MARY DOWNING HAHN

AN AVON  CAMELOT BOOK

AVON BOOKS, INC.
1350 Avenue of the Americas
New York, New York 10019

Copyright © 1991 by Mary Downing Hahn
Published by arrangement with Clarion Books, a Houghton Mifflin Company imprint
Library of Congress Catalog Card Number: 91-7706
ISBN: 0-380-71900-2
www.avonbooks.com

First Avon Camelot Printing: October 1992
First Avon Camelot Special Printing: September 1992

CAMELOT TRADEMARK REG. U.S. PAT. OFF. AND IN OTHER COUNTRIES, MARCA REGISTRADA, HECHO EN U.S.A.

Printed in the U.S.A.

This book is dedicated to the Downing family:

Especially to the memory of
my father, Kenneth Ernest Downing (1904–63),

and my uncles:

Dudley Downing, who was killed in Belgium in 1944 and
awarded the Distinguished Service
Cross for exceptional heroism in combat,

and

William Alexander Downing, who survived the
Battle of the Bulge in the Ardennes forest.

STEPPING
ON
THE CRACKS

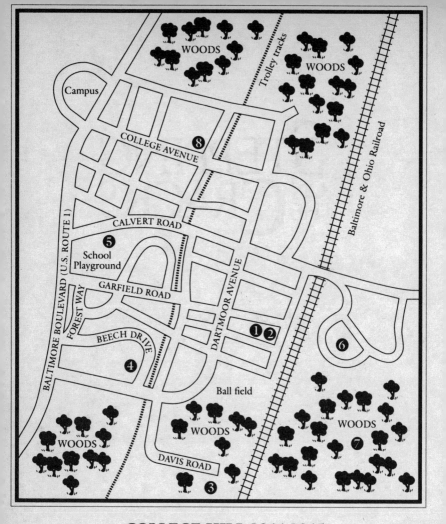

COLLEGE HILL 1944-1945

1 Elizabeth's house
2 Margaret's house
3 Gordy's house
4 Barbara's house
5 College Hill Elementary School
6 Experimental farm
7 Gordy's hut
8 Trolley Stoppe Shoppe

1

*O*ne afternoon in August, Elizabeth and I were sprawled on my front porch playing an endless game of Monopoly (or Monotony, as Elizabeth called it).

"Your turn," I announced. I'd just passed the bank and picked up two hundred dollars to add to my pile of paper money. For once, I was definitely winning.

When she drew a card that told her to go to jail, Elizabeth threw it down. She was already broke and in debt to me because I owned Atlantic Place and her man kept landing on it. Every time that happened, she had to hand me five hundred dollars rent.

Elizabeth scowled at her little pile of money and ran a hand through her blonde hair, putting a few more tangles in it. Then she poked the Monopoly board with one bare foot, just hard enough to slide the expensive hotels and cottages off my property. Our little men rolled across the porch, and some of the paper money fluttered away.

"Let's go somewhere before I keel over and die of boredom," Elizabeth said.

Ignoring her, I crawled around, gathering up the playing pieces. Unlike Elizabeth, I was perfectly content to spend the rest of the day where we were. The heat had melted my bones away, and I felt as limp as a rag doll. "It's too hot," I muttered, "to do anything."

But Elizabeth wasn't listening. Climbing to the porch railing, she grinned down at me. "Dare me to jump?"

Before I could say yes or no, Elizabeth hollered "Geronimo!" Arching her body, she flew through the air like a circus acrobat and landed gracefully on the grass. "Come on, Margaret," she shouted.

Not wanting to be a sissy baby, I held my breath, leapt off the railing, and hit the ground so hard I knocked the scab off my skinned knee. As I spit on my finger to wipe the blood away, Elizabeth hopped down the sidewalk.

"Step on a crack," she yelled, "break Hitler's back! Step on a crack, break Hitler's back!"

Despite the heat, I stamped along behind Elizabeth. Under my bare feet, I saw Hitler's face on the cement— his beady eyes, his mustache, his mean little slit of a mouth. I shouted and pounded him into the pavement, and every time I said his name it was like swearing. It was Hitler's fault my brother Jimmy was in the army, Hitler's fault Mother cried when she thought I wouldn't hear, Hitler's fault Daddy never laughed or told jokes, Hitler's fault, Hitler's fault, Hitler's most horrible fault. I hated him and his Nazis with a passion so strong and deep it scared me.

Behind me, the screen door opened, and Mother called, "Margaret, how often do I have to tell you not to jump like that?" She frowned at me from the porch. "You won't be happy till you ruin your insides, will you?"

Elizabeth grinned at Mother, her eyes squinted against the sun. "Hi, Mrs. Baker," she said.

Mother looked at Elizabeth, but she didn't return her smile. "What was all that shouting?" she asked. "You two were making enough noise to wake the dead."

"It's a game I thought up," Elizabeth said. "Step on a crack," she yelled, jumping hard on the sidewalk to demonstrate. "Break Hitler's back!"

"When I was your age, we said, 'Step on a crack, break your *mother's* back,' " Mother told her. "We tried hard *not* to step on the cracks."

"That was before Hitler," Elizabeth said. "The world was different then."

Mother leaned against the door frame, her arms folded across her chest, and sighed. "Yes," she said, agreeing for once with Elizabeth. "I guess it was."

For a moment or two, no one said anything. I saw Mother glance at the blue star hanging in our living room window, and I knew what she was thinking. That star meant Jimmy was overseas fighting a war Hitler started. There was a star in Elizabeth's window, too, because her brother Joe was in the Navy. That summer, there were stars in lots of windows in College Hill, and not all of them were blue. Some, like the one across the street in the Bedfords' window, were gold. The Bedfords' son Harold had been killed in Italy last summer. That was what gold meant.

In the silence, I heard a surge of organ music from our radio. It was time for "The Romance of Helen Trent," one of Mother's favorite soap operas. As she opened the screen door to go inside, Mother paused and looked at Elizabeth. "Where are you two going this afternoon?" she asked.

"Bike riding," Elizabeth said, as if I'd already agreed.

"Don't you dare take Margaret down that hill on Beech Drive," Mother said. "You almost killed yourselves last time."

3

But she was speaking to the air. Elizabeth had already darted through a gap in the hedge between our houses. In a few seconds she was back with her brother Joe's bike, an old Schwinn. The crossbar was so high Elizabeth could barely straddle it, but she rode it anyway.

Taking my seat on the carrier over the rear wheel, I held on to Elizabeth's waist as she pushed off across the grass. Wobbling till she picked up speed, she pedaled along Garfield Road toward Dartmoor Avenue.

The hot sunlight poured down through the green leaves, dappling the dirt road with a lacy pattern of shadows, and the Schwinn's big balloon tires bounced over the ruts. Mrs. Bedford waved to us from her front porch, Mrs. Porter smiled at us from her side yard, where she was hanging her laundry out to dry, and old Mr. Zimmerman nodded to us from the corner. His little dog, Major, barked and wagged his tail. On a cooler day, he might have chased us.

Through the open windows of every house, we heard snatches of radio shows. The voice of Helen Trent and the happy song advertising Rinso laundry soap followed us down the shady street. College Hill was so peaceful, it was easy to forget the war. In fact, Helen Trent's love life seemed more real than the battles our parents talked about. Although it was 1944, and World War II had been going on for over two and a half years, nothing had happened to change our lives. Except for Jimmy's absence and a lot of shortages, everything was the way it had always been.

With me clinging behind her, Elizabeth crossed the trolley tracks and pedaled past the school, sleeping like a brick giant in the summer sunlight. Soon enough its green doors would open wide and swallow us up, but for now we were safe. Three more weeks of freedom before we faced sixth grade and the dreaded Mrs. Wagner.

Elizabeth turned a corner, and we glided down Forest Way toward Beech Drive. The road here was paved, and Elizabeth pedaled faster, zooming past big brick houses with mossy slate roofs. The bike tires made a hissing sound on the gritty surface of the macadam, and a dog barked at us from behind a picket fence. Otherwise, it was very quiet.

Not far from Beech Drive, Elizabeth's back tensed and she braked hard. "Oh, no," she said. "Not him."

Looking over her shoulder, I saw what she saw. Just ahead, three bicycles blocked the street. Gordy and his friends, Toad and Doug, were waiting for us. From two blocks away, I could see the sneers on their faces.

If there was anybody in College Hill I hated more than Gordy Smith, I didn't know who it was. Way back in kindergarten, the very first time he ever saw Elizabeth, Gordy had walked right up to her and pulled her hair as hard as he could. Being Elizabeth, she'd punched him in the stomach. They'd been enemies ever since. Because I was Elizabeth's best friend, I was on her side against Gordy.

For some reason, Gordy was meaner than ever this summer. You'd think he was a Nazi, the way he acted, fighting with everyone and picking on girls and little kids. The very sight of him scared me to death, and I scrunched down behind Elizabeth.

"Turn around," I whispered, squeezing her waist to get her attention. "Go back the way we came. Maybe Gordy won't bother us."

Elizabeth tried to swerve down a side street, but, with

me behind her, she wasn't fast enough. In seconds, the three boys had us surrounded.

"Well, well, if it isn't Little Lizard," Gordy said. He was wearing a dented Civil Defense warden's helmet, a striped jersey, stretched at the neck and several sizes too small, and old knickers held up with suspenders. Pure meanness shone out of his gray eyes.

Elizabeth gripped the bike's handlebars so tightly her knuckles turned white. "Don't call me Lizard," she said. "My name is E-liz-a-beth!"

"I'll call you anything I like, *Lizard.*" Gordy grabbed her handlebars with one hand and smirked at her. Then he looked at me.

"Hey, Baby Magpie. Cat got your tongue as usual?" Grabbing one of my braids, he tugged just hard enough to pull me toward him. As I tried to yank free, he laughed and let me go, and I bounced back behind Elizabeth.

In the silence, Doug blew a big bubble, popped it loudly, and sucked it slowly back into his mouth. He was short, and his skin was almost exactly the same color as the dirty blonde hair that hung in his eyes.

"Hey, Gordy," he said. "You better listen to E-liz-a-beth. She's one tough cookie."

Toad didn't say anything. He just looked at Gordy and giggled. In the heat, his face was as red as his hair, and his freckles had gotten so dark he looked like a fat leopard.

Gordy leaned toward Elizabeth and said, "We just got a letter from Donald. He's blowing Nazi planes out of the sky." He pretended he was pointing a gun at her. "Ackety, ackety, ack."

Some of his spit shot past Elizabeth and sprayed my

cheek. I made a face and rubbed it away, but Gordy didn't notice.

"I bet your brother hasn't killed half as many Japs," Gordy said to Elizabeth. "Donald's the best gunner in the whole army. When Toad and Doug and me are old enough, we're going to be just like him. We'll kill lots of Nazis. Maybe even Hitler himself."

"You dumbo, the war will be over way before you grow up," Elizabeth said scornfully.

Gordy shoved his face close to hers, and Elizabeth drew back, tense again. "Girls don't know diddley squat about war, so don't act smart, Lizard."

"Let go of my bike," Elizabeth said.

Gordy shook the handlebars. "This is Joe's bike."

"Well, let go of it anyway!" Elizabeth tried to pry Gordy's fingers off.

"Oh, Dougie," he yelped, "help me. Lizard's hurting me so bad."

They all laughed and moved their bikes even closer to us. Gordy leaned toward Elizabeth again. He was so near, I could smell peanut butter and something less pleasant on his breath. His black hair hung in his eyes, he had a pimple in the corner of his mouth, and his neck was circled with a dark ring of dirt. "Give me a kiss, Lizard," he said. "Then I'll let you go."

"I'd rather kiss a pig," Elizabeth said. "They smell better."

When Gordy leaned even closer, puckering his lips and making loud smooching sounds, Elizabeth pulled back, bumping her head against mine. "Get away from me," she yelled. "You stink."

7

Just as Gordy grabbed Elizabeth's arm, Mrs. Fuller stepped out on the front porch of the house on the corner. "That's enough, Gordon Smith," she called. "You leave those girls alone."

"Why don't you mind your own beeswax?" Gordy yelled at her. "Old busybody." But he dropped Elizabeth's arm. Then, spinning his tires on loose pebbles, he zoomed off down the street with Doug and Toad flanking him.

"Hey, Lizard," he called back, "you got away this time, but there's always a next time. I'll be looking for you!"

Mrs. Fuller stood on her porch and watched the boys disappear around a corner, laughing and yelling insults at her, Elizabeth, and me.

"I don't know what the world's coming to," she said to no one in particular. "Children run wild these days, with no respect for anyone." Frowning at Elizabeth and me, she went inside, letting her screen door slam behind her.

"I wish Gordy was old enough to get drafted," I said as Elizabeth began pedaling toward home. "Then we wouldn't ever have to see him again."

"Me, too," Elizabeth agreed. "I hate him so much I wouldn't care if the Nazis dropped a bomb on him. *Kapow!*"

"You sure told him off," I said.

She grinned at me over her shoulder. "I should've slapped him. In the movies, Joan Crawford always wallops guys who get fresh with her."

Standing up, Elizabeth pumped harder. A little breeze fanned my cheeks, but rivulets of sweat ran down her backbone, streaking her blue jersey. Resting on the seat,

Elizabeth let the bike coast, and we rolled silently around the corner and down Garfield Road.

Glancing behind me at the empty street, I hoped we wouldn't see Gordy again till school started. But in a town as small as College Hill, it's hard to avoid people, especially if they're looking for you.

2

*W*hen Mother saw me coming up the back steps, she said, "Sit down and rest, Margaret. You look like you're about to have heat stroke."

Taking the glass of ice water she handed me, I perched on the kitchen counter and watched her iron. She had one of Daddy's tan work shirts spread out on the board, so stiff with starch she had to pry it off when she was done. The little Philco radio on top of the refrigerator was tuned to "The Guiding Light," another one of her favorite soap operas.

As the episode ended, Mother turned to me. "Where did you and Elizabeth go today?"

"Just around. Not very far." I drank the last of my water and started crunching an ice cube. "We saw Gordy," I added. "He's so ugly. Elizabeth and I hate his guts."

Mother looked up from a pair of Daddy's work pants. "Don't talk like that, Margaret," she said.

"Why not? He's horrible and disgusting, and he spit all over me."

Mother frowned and pressed the iron on Daddy's pants so hard they steamed, releasing the sweet smell of starch mixed with a kind of burning odor. Lifting the iron, she frowned at the tiny singe mark on the cloth. "Ladies don't use words like 'guts,' " she said. "Do you want people to think you have no manners?"

"Well, I don't think it's good manners for somebody to spit on another person."

Mother sighed and brushed a strand of gray hair out of her eyes. "Try to have a little sympathy for people like Gordy," she said. "Suppose you lived the way he does. Or had a father like Mr. Smith."

I swung my heels against the cabinet door and watched Mother sprinkle more water on Daddy's pants. I'd never met Gordy's father, but I'd learned a lot about him from Elizabeth. Her father was a policeman, and he'd arrested Mr. Smith more than once for being drunk and disorderly. Elizabeth wasn't supposed to know things like that, but, being a good listener, she heard plenty of stories about the nights Mr. Smith got drunk at the Starlight Tavern and started fights. In Mr. Crawford's opinion, Mr. Smith was a no-good bum, and he wished he'd take his family and get out of town. "Poor white trash, the lot of them," Mr. Crawford said.

A couple of times, when Elizabeth and I were feeling brave, we'd ridden Joe's bike down Davis Road, right past Gordy's house, hoping to get a glimpse of Mr. Smith. The yard was full of broken toys and all sorts of junk. Grubby little Smiths, smaller versions of Gordy, yelled at us from behind the fence. Sometimes they even threw things.

But I didn't think Gordy's house or his father were any excuse for his behavior. He was mean and ugly and, no matter what Mother had to say about my choice of language, I hated his guts.

"Margaret, please stop kicking the cabinet," Mother said. A pair of my shorts lay on the ironing board, and she was frowning at the grass stains on the seat.

"Can't you be more careful?" she asked. "It's hard

enough these days just replacing the things you grow out of. It makes me mad to see you ruin perfectly good clothes."

"I'm sorry," I said. Putting my empty glass in the sink, I left the kitchen. Sometimes I couldn't please my mother no matter what I said or did. It seemed to me she'd been in a bad mood ever since Jimmy was drafted.

*

A few hours later, I was sitting on the front porch looking at cartoons in the *Saturday Evening Post*. Hearing footsteps, I looked up and saw Daddy trudging toward me. He'd walked two blocks from the trolley stop, and his forehead was beaded with perspiration. Even though he worked in Washington fixing other people's Buicks, we couldn't afford a car ourselves. Gas and tires were just too expensive.

Grunting his usual hello, Daddy walked past me without even giving me a pat on the head. As the screen door shut behind him, I heard him ask Mother if we'd gotten a letter from Jimmy.

I sat there for a few minutes, staring at the magazine cover. Daddy was going to be disappointed. I'd waited all morning for the mail, hoping for a letter, but Mr. Murphy had handed me the telephone bill, the electric bill, and the magazine I was holding now. He'd felt bad, I could tell. It must be awful to walk up people's sidewalks knowing you haven't got the letters they're waiting for.

Riffling the pages of the magazine to find more cartoons, I told myself a letter from Jimmy would come tomorrow. Maybe even three or four. It happened that way sometimes.

"Margaret," Mother called. "Dinner's ready."

Taking my place at the table, I poked at my food. "Not stew again," I said.

Daddy frowned at me. "Think of the starving children in France and Holland," he said, "and be glad you have a roof over your head and something to eat."

Silently I choked down the stew. I didn't want to think about those children. *Life* magazine was full of their pictures, skinny, frightened little kids peering from the bombed-out ruins of their homes. "Why them," I sometimes asked myself, "and not me?"

After we'd finished eating, Daddy lit a cigarette and spread the *Evening Star* on the table beside his plate. Smoke drifted past my nose and prickled my eyes, but I stayed in my chair and tried to see what he was reading.

"Things look good, Lil," he said after a while. "Everybody says we'll be in Paris before September. The war should be over in the fall. We're breaking Hitler's back at last."

Thinking about Elizabeth's and my game, I grinned at Daddy. I wanted to tell him about all the cracks we'd stamped on, but he wasn't looking at me. He was staring through a cloud of cigarette smoke at something only he could see.

"Wouldn't it be wonderful if Jimmy was home for Christmas this year?" he asked Mother.

She smiled at Daddy and squeezed my hand. For a moment we sat quietly, thinking about Jimmy, imagining him with us, a whole family, four people at the table, laughter and jokes again. I glanced at his picture on the sideboard, a soldier smiling at us from a silver frame.

"We'll have turkey," Mother said, "and sweet potatoes,

cranberries, pumpkin pie made with real butter, all the sugar and coffee we want." Her voice trailed off happily as she began clearing the table.

When I went upstairs to bed, the heat was lying in wait, stifling me with the smell of mothballs, old wool, and furniture polish. Yearning for a breeze, I pressed my face against the window screen, but the air outside was just as hot and still as it was inside. On the horizon, just above the shaggy treetops, heat lightning flickered dimly across the sky, and thunder muttered like artillery fire in the distance.

A mile down the tracks, a train blew its whistle for the Calvert Road crossing. Nearer and nearer it came, its whistle wailing louder and louder, its engine thundering, its wheels pounding against the tracks, filling the night with noise. As the locomotive rumbled past the end of our yard, it shook the whole house, jiggled my bed, rattled the glass in my window, and made my collection of china animals clink against each other.

Then, as quickly as it came, the train roared away toward Baltimore, blowing its whistle for the next crossing. In the sudden silence it left behind, I heard the crickets chirping in the bushes and Mother's and Daddy's voices in the living room.

Too hot to sleep, I pulled my scrapbook down from a shelf in my closet. Ever since Jimmy was drafted, I'd been keeping things about the war to show him when he came home. I saved cartoons and all the *Saturday Evening Post* covers with pictures of Private Willie Gillis. Willie looked sort of like Jimmy, and I thought he probably had the same personality. I could imagine him telling jokes and getting into a little trouble every now and then.

Jimmy's letters to me were in my scrapbook, too. He always started them "Dear Princess Maggie May" and then told me funny things that happened to him and drew pictures to go with them. He was a good artist, and he made me think the war might not be so bad after all. At least not for him. The potatoes he peeled, the latrines he cleaned, the terrible food, the dumb sergeants. You didn't die of things like that, you just laughed them off and hoped the war would end soon.

After I read all the letters, I felt better. Like Willie Gillis, Jimmy was safe somewhere in a foxhole in France or Belgium. How could anyone, even a Nazi, want to hurt my brother?

Putting my scrapbook away, I turned out my light and prayed to God to keep my brother safe. Then I sank down into a dream that the war was over and Jimmy was home and we were on our way to Ocean City in a brand-new car. Like a family on a magazine cover, we were happy. There was nothing for Daddy to get mad about or me to cry over. With Jimmy telling jokes to make us laugh, even flat tires and melted ice cream were funny.

A couple of days later, Elizabeth and I were sitting on a platform we'd built in the oak tree at the end of my yard, as far from the house as we could get. Out of our mothers' sight, we were less likely to be called inside to help with boring chores. According to Elizabeth, it was a known fact that people didn't think to look up when they were searching for someone.

From where we sat, we could see Mother picking tomatoes in our Victory Garden. She was proud of all the vegetables we'd grown. It was one of our contributions to the war effort, she told me, like saving scrap and buying bonds. Anything we could do to help our country helped Jimmy, so she worked in the garden every day, weeding and watering, keeping the rows as neat and straight as a picture.

The back of Mother's flowered housedress was dark with sweat, and she paused every now and then to swat at the mosquitoes circling her head. I knew I should go down and help her, but the heat drained my energy. Wisps of hair escaped from my braids and stuck to my neck, and my jersey felt like it was wallpapered to my skin.

"What do you want to do?" I asked Elizabeth.

"I don't know." Elizabeth caught a ladybug and

watched it crawl up her arm. That was how bored she was.

"We could play paper dolls," I suggested. "Or Monopoly."

"Not me." Elizabeth blew on the ladybug, and it flew away. "Hurry up," she said. "Your house is on fire and your children will burn."

Yawning, she picked up a Captain Marvel comic book and turned the pages idly, barely looking at the pictures. She was wearing a ruffled top and a pair of white shorts with red bands on the side seams. In an outfit like hers, I would have looked like a walking skeleton. Even with a jersey on, each bone in my spine stuck out like a knob.

Suddenly Elizabeth pressed a finger against her lips. "Shhh," she whispered and pointed behind me.

Peering through the leaves, I saw Gordy, Doug, and Toad coming down the alley. Gordy had gotten a real army helmet from somewhere, and he and Doug were carrying Daisy air rifles, the kind I'd seen advertised in comic books. Toad was wearing Gordy's old Civil Defense helmet, but his only weapon was a Roy Rogers cap pistol. They were pretending to be commandos, I think, running from garage to garage, signaling each other, crouching behind garbage cans. Every now and then, one of them would lob a rock at something and make an exploding grenade sound.

"What dumbos," Elizabeth hissed in my ear.

I nodded, too scared to say anything. The boys had come to a halt right under us. I could see the dented top of Gordy's army helmet and the crooked part in Doug's hair. Holding my breath, I clung to a limb, waiting for them to move on, but they knelt in the alley and pointed their guns at a thicket in the corner of our yard.

"Come out of there, you dirty Nazi," Gordy shouted at an imaginary enemy.

Then Elizabeth did a really stupid thing. Grabbing an acorn, she aimed carefully and dropped it on Gordy's helmet. "Bombs away!" she yelled. "The sky is falling, the sky is falling!"

Startled, Gordy looked up and spotted us in the tree. Vaulting the sagging fence, he grabbed one of the boards we'd nailed to the trunk and started climbing toward us.

Like monkeys, Elizabeth and I scrambled higher into the branches, but Gordy caught Elizabeth's foot and yanked so hard she almost lost her grip and fell.

"Let go!" She kicked at him with her other foot, landing a bare foot on his helmet with a satisfying thud.

While I watched from above, Toad and Doug joined Gordy on the platform. I heard it creak under their weight.

"Look, comics," Doug said. "The spoils of war." He picked them up and started sorting through them. The ones he didn't like, he tore apart page by page and tossed off the platform. Angrily, I watched Porky Pig, Archie, Little Lulu, and Bugs Bunny drift down like leaves and land on the tangle of honeysuckle and poison ivy covering the fence.

"Bombs away, Lizard," Gordy said as another handful of colored pages rustled toward the ground.

"Mother!" I screamed from high in the tree. "Mother, help!"

But Mother didn't answer. Except for a lone black crow stalking up and down the rows of vegetables, the Victory

Garden was deserted. From inside the house, she would never hear me yelling.

"Hey, Magpie, shut up," Gordy said, "or I'll shoot you full of BBs."

I looked down at him, and, sure enough, he was aiming his air rifle right at my rear end. If any boy would do something like that, Gordy would.

"We can use these boards," Gordy said to Doug and Toad. While we watched, too scared of the air rifles to protest, the boys began tearing our platform apart. The nails screamed as they came loose, and the boards clattered down to the alley.

"Girls can't build anything right," Gordy said as he yanked the last board free and tossed it on the pile. It took him less than five minutes to destroy what Elizabeth and I had spent hours constructing. "I bet they don't even know which end of a hammer to hit the nail with."

"I'm telling Joe when he gets home," Elizabeth said. "He'll come over to your house and beat you up."

"Oh, Lizard, I'm so scared," Gordy said, pitching his voice into a high falsetto.

"I hate you!" she yelled. "You're worse than a Nazi!"

"Geronimo," Gordy shouted and jumped out of the tree like a parachuter. On the ground, he helped Doug and Toad collect the scattered boards and comics.

"We were spotting enemy planes from up here," Elizabeth screamed at them, "and you sabotaged us. That makes you a dirty, rotten traitor!"

"Shut up, Lizard, or I'll climb up there and—" Watching Elizabeth all the time, Gordy whispered the rest of his threat to Doug and Toad. They all laughed and whooped.

"Only a tree trunk between you and me, Lizard!"

Gordy shouted. Then he and his two friends leapt down the bank and ran across the train tracks, carrying our boards and comics with them.

Shaking with rage, I watched them disappear into the woods on the other side. "If only a train would come along and smash them to smithereens!"

"Especially Gordy," Elizabeth muttered. "Just little parts of him would be left. A finger, a toe, a tooth. They could bury him in a teacup."

She dropped down from the tree, and I scrambled after her. "Just wait," Elizabeth said as we began picking up the remains of our comics. "We'll get even with Gordy for this."

While her back was turned, I shook my head. I didn't have any idea what sort of revenge she was planning, but I wasn't going to have any part of it. In my opinion, the farther we stayed from Gordy the safer we'd be, but I knew better than to argue with Elizabeth. The best thing to do was to keep quiet and hope she'd forget about Gordy.

I should have known better. For days after Gordy wrecked our tree house, Elizabeth talked of nothing but getting even with him, but luckily she couldn't come up with a plan. Which was fine with me. I sure didn't want to make Gordy hate us more than he already did.

*

About a week later, Elizabeth and I were sitting in our tree. We'd tried to rebuild our platform twice, but every time we nailed it together, the boards disappeared. We were sure Gordy was taking them, but we never caught him in the act. At least he couldn't tear down the tree. We still had a private place to sit and talk.

While Elizabeth was telling me every detail of a scary "Inner Sanctum" show she'd heard, a troop train roared past, drowning out her voice. There were lots of cars, and Elizabeth and I leaned out of the tree to wave to the soldiers.

"Just think," Elizabeth said, "they might remember us when they're in their tanks or hiding in their foxholes. 'Those girls who waved,' they'll say, 'we're making the world safe for them.' "

I nodded, but I was thinking about Jimmy. Every soldier I saw reminded me of him. We'd finally gotten three letters, all on the same day, just as I'd thought we might. Although Jimmy said he was fine, he hadn't put in any jokes. In my letter, he told me he missed me and drew a picture of himself carrying me piggyback. Under it, he'd written, "I hope you won't be too big for this when I come home." I noticed I looked smaller in the picture than I really am, and I realized I'd gotten taller since Jimmy left.

"I hope they all come home safe," Elizabeth said, as the last car rumbled past.

Silently we watched the train shrink to a speck and vanish down the tracks. It was going north toward Baltimore, Philadelphia, New York, carrying the soldiers to ships that would take them across the ocean to England and France, to Italy and Belgium, and someday maybe to Germany itself.

"If you were a boy," Elizabeth said to me, "would you want to go to war?"

"Would you?"

"Of course." Elizabeth gave me a fierce look. "I wouldn't be scared. I'd be a hero."

I bent my head to scratch a mosquito bite on my leg. If

I had to go to war, I'd probably fall down on the battlefield and pretend to be dead till they stopped shooting. Unlike Elizabeth, I was a chicken through and through, and everybody, including her, knew it.

Suddenly Elizabeth poked me hard in the ribs. "Look who I see."

Too far away to notice us in the tree, Gordy, Doug, and Toad were running across the tracks, dressed as soldiers as usual. Silently we watched them scramble up the opposite bank and disappear into the woods.

"They must be going to that hut of theirs," Elizabeth muttered. For a moment she sat still, one hand curled around a limb, staring at the trees. Then she turned to me. "Let's follow them and find out where it is. Maybe we could get our boards back. Wouldn't that be a great revenge?"

I stared at her, scared speechless. For one thing, my parents didn't allow me to cross the train tracks, but, more than that, I was terrified of Gordy. What if he caught us down there in the woods? Who would hear or see? Who would rescue us?

Unfortunately, Elizabeth didn't wait for me to agree or disagree. Assuming I'd follow her, she swung down from the tree and ran to the top of the railroad bank.

When Elizabeth looked back to see where I was, she frowned. I was still sitting in the tree, clinging to a limb and wishing I had her nerve. Elizabeth was our favorite comic strip heroines, Wonder Woman, Mary Marvel, and Cat Woman, all rolled up in one. Nothing scared her. Not leaping from trees, not crossing the train tracks. Not even going into lonely, forbidden places where tramps lurked and boys like Gordy crept from tree to tree, armed with air rifles, just looking for girls like us.

"Come on, sissy baby!" Elizabeth yelled.

Reluctantly, I backed down the tree trunk, my legs and arms rubbery with fear. If Elizabeth was brave enough to go into the woods, I would go with her.

4

*B*y the time I got to the top of the bank, Elizabeth was waving at me from the tracks. The steel rails stretched out of sight in both directions, northbound to Baltimore and southbound to Washington, wavering in the heat. Two blocks away was the little yellow train station and just beyond it was Calvert Road, the only crossing in College Hill.

While I hesitated, an old black car rattled across the tracks and disappeared behind a line of trees, leaving a dust cloud behind. Nothing else stirred. College Hill slept in the afternoon heat. Not even Mr. Zimmerman and Major were in sight.

"Come on, Chicken Little," Elizabeth called up to me. She was balanced on a rail, tense with impatience.

Cautiously, I slid down the bank, feeling the cinders roll out from under my feet. "You know we're not allowed to cross the train tracks," I told her.

Shading her eyes with one hand, Elizabeth peered this way and that. "Is there a mother in the house?" she called. Scrambling up the other bank, she grinned at me from the top. "No mothers anywhere in sight."

Smarting under Elizabeth's scorn, I scampered across the shining tracks and blundered up the grassy bank. Elizabeth was ahead of me, running across the field toward the woods, and I dashed after her, anxious to catch up.

A barbed wire fence stopped us for a moment. Old and rusty, it sagged to the ground. Elizabeth hopped over it, but I hesitated. On one strand of wire was a sign. "Private Property. No Trespassing," I read. It was shot full of holes.

"What about this sign?" I asked Elizabeth.

"Don't worry about it," she said. "Nobody owns these woods. At least nobody we know."

Cautiously, I stepped over the sagging wire, afraid of scratching my legs. Rust gave you blood poisoning if you cut yourself. You got lockjaw and died a horrible death.

Safely over the fence, I peered into the woods ahead. Everything was still and green and damp. A buzzing cloud of gnats circled my head, a woodpecker knocked away at a tree, a crow cawed. I was sure Gordy, Doug, and Toad were hiding in the bushes, watching us right now, aiming their air rifles at our hearts.

"Follow me," Elizabeth whispered, "and don't make any noise."

Wondering why I always let Elizabeth lead me into danger, I crept through the woods behind her. Every time I stepped on a twig, she turned and said, "Shush!" Before long, I felt like Small at the end of Pooh's long line of explorers in search of the North Pole. I was being shushed all the time, but there was no one for *me* to shush. It wasn't fair.

Suddenly, I heard voices, and Elizabeth dropped to the ground. Following her example, I flopped down on my stomach and lay there, limp with fear. Not far away, barely visible through the underbrush, was a small hut. It had two windows with real glass in them and a crooked chimney poking out of its roof. A few feet from the door, Gordy, Doug, and Toad were sitting on a log in a clearing, smoking cigarettes. The trees cast a mottled shade over them as a breeze stirred the leaves.

"Can you hear what they're saying?" Elizabeth whispered to me.

When I shook my head, she said, "If we sneak up to that tree, we can listen to every word."

Commando style, she crept toward a tall oak with a reassuringly thick trunk, and I crawled after her. The closer we got, the louder my heart thumped.

"Okay, stop," Elizabeth whispered.

I lay flat and tried to breathe normally. The dusty smell of tree bark tickled my nose, and I shifted away from it, afraid I might sneeze.

Gordy was wearing his army helmet and a pair of baggy shorts. The cigarette dangling from his lower lip made him seem older and even meaner than usual. Just looking at him made me feel weak.

"There's no Nazi plane that can come close to a B-24," Doug was saying. "My cousin Harry flies one, and he ought to know."

"How about a panzer, though?" Gordy asked. "Our tanks aren't as good as them."

"What are you, some kind of Hitler lover?" Toad asked. "Everything we have is better than German junk. That's why we'll win. We're the best."

For at least ten minutes, Elizabeth and I eavesdropped on the most boring conversation I'd ever heard in my life. All the boys did was argue about which planes, tanks, submarines, guns, bombs, and hand grenades were best.

I nudged Elizabeth a couple of times, trying to signal her to leave, but she seemed to be hanging on every word the boys said. Wearily, I waited for something to happen.

Anything would be better than lying in the weeds with ants crawling up and down my bare legs.

Finally Doug said, "Okay, which pinup do you like best?"

"Betty Grable," Toad said. "That picture of her looking over her shoulder. You know, in the bathing suit and high heels."

"Nah," Gordy said. "Rita Hayworth gets my vote. She's really sexy."

"How about Jane Russell?" Doug said. "She's got the biggest chest." He stood up and cupped his hands to demonstrate. "Hubba, hubba," he said and wiggled his hips.

I don't know how long they would have laughed if I hadn't finally sneezed. That dusty smell had tickled and tugged at my nose, making it itch till I couldn't stand it.

Gordy jumped to his feet and yelled, and Elizabeth and I ran off through the woods, ducking and dodging trees and low limbs. A branch whipped my face hard enough to bring tears to my eyes, brambles slashed my legs, I stumbled over something and almost fell. But I kept on going, and so did Elizabeth.

Behind us, I heard the boys crashing through the bushes, shouting and calling us names. They'd kill us if they caught us, I was sure of it.

Just as we reached the fence, Doug grabbed my jersey and yanked me backward. "Let me go," I cried, wiggling and twisting, trying to break free. "Let me go!"

"What the hell are you girls doing down here?" Gordy yelled at Elizabeth. He caught her wrists. The jugular vein in his neck pulsed, and the jagged scar over his eyebrow was purple against his pale skin.

"You took our boards," Elizabeth shouted. Her face was

red with anger, and her hair blazed like white fire in the hot sunlight. "We want them back!"

Gordy held her wrists tighter and sneered at her. "You just can't stay away from me, can you, Lizard?"

"Don't call me that!" Elizabeth yelled. Drawing back one leg, she kicked Gordy in the shins hard enough to make him wince.

"I wouldn't try that again, *Lizard*," Gordy said. He paused a moment and glanced at me. Then, pitching his voice lower, he said, "You little dopes don't know it, but I just saved your miserable lives. Not that I expect either one of you to thank me for it."

"What are you talking about?" Elizabeth asked. "Are you nuts or something?"

"Haven't you heard about the crazy man who lives in these woods? Hasn't anybody warned you?" Gordy looked at Elizabeth scornfully.

"Liar," Elizabeth said. "There's no crazy man around here."

"He was standing right behind you with a knife in his hand," Gordy said. "But you were so busy spying on us you didn't even notice."

"Where is he now?" Elizabeth was doing her best to sound as sassy as she had before, but I could hear a little uncertainty creeping into her voice.

As for me, I was so scared my saliva dried up. My mouth felt like sand, and I didn't think I could say a word, let alone scream for help.

"He ran when he saw us coming," Gordy went on, "just because he was outnumbered."

"I don't believe you," Elizabeth said. She looked at Toad

and Doug, but they were nodding their heads, backing up Gordy.

"You girls better stay out of the woods," Gordy said. "I might not be here to save you next time."

"I've never heard anyone say there was a crazy man down here," Elizabeth persisted. The boys had let go of us by now, but we stayed where we were, waiting to hear what Gordy would say next.

"That's because it's top secret, Lizard," Gordy said. "You know the experimental farm over there?" He pointed across the field at a cluster of brick buildings owned by the state university, and Elizabeth nodded. She kept her eyes, slightly narrowed, on Gordy's face, but I had the feeling she was beginning to believe in the crazy man.

"Well, those scientists don't just do stuff for the university," he went on. "They get army contracts sometimes. They were working with chemicals to see if they could make men braver and stronger, better soldiers or something, but the guy they were experimenting on went crazy. They couldn't control him. They kept him locked up for a while in one of the stables, but a couple of weeks ago he broke out. He's loose in the woods, and he'll kill anyone he gets his hands on. He's got a knife this long." Gordy held his hands about two feet apart.

"That's what he was coming after you with!" he shouted, and I was so startled, I jumped at least six inches straight up in the air.

"So you better stay away from here, see?" Gordy shoved his face so close to Elizabeth's she stumbled backward.

"Why don't they catch him?" she asked.

"Don't you think they've tried?" Gordy looked over his shoulder at the silent woods. "It's a jungle back there," he whispered, "and the crazy man is real smart. He can just disappear into the underbrush. You don't know where he is until—" Gordy gave a bloodcurdling scream and grabbed Elizabeth around the neck "—he's got you!"

As scary as Gordy's scream was, something else terrified me even more. Without waiting for Elizabeth or anyone else, I leapt the fence and took off across the field as fast as I could, yelling at the top of my lungs. Hurtling down the railroad bank, I ran across the tracks without even looking for a train, scrambled up the other side, and raced down the alley toward home.

Elizabeth caught up with me before I'd gotten to the back gate. Grabbing my arm, she stopped me from running straight into the house and telling Mother everything.

"Don't believe Gordy," she said. "He's just making it up to scare us away from his stupid hut."

"What are you talking about?" I yelled. "Didn't you see him?"

Elizabeth stared at me. "See who?"

"The crazy man. Just before Gordy screamed. He was hiding, watching us. His hair was all shaggy, and he was dressed in rags. I saw him, I saw him!"

And I had, I wasn't making it up, I'd seen the crazy man in the woods. Just a glimpse and then he was gone, like Gordy said, melting away into the leaves and shadows.

Elizabeth shook her head impatiently. "Nobody was there," she insisted. "Gordy was lying."

"No!" I was crying now. "I saw him."

"Well, you must be nuts, then," Elizabeth said. "Seeing things that don't exist. That's a sign of going cuckoo." She pointed a finger at the side of her head and twirled it.

I bit my lip hard to stop myself from crying. I didn't want Elizabeth to think I was crazy. "Just because you didn't see him doesn't mean *I* didn't," I said.

Elizabeth sighed. She'd lost both barrettes in the woods, and her hair spilled over her eyes like wisps of cotton. "Believe what you want," she said. "I know a lie when I hear one."

Before I could say anything more, Mrs. Crawford opened the kitchen door and spotted us. "Elizabeth," she called. "Time for chores."

With her back to her mother, Elizabeth twisted her face into a hideous grimace. "I have to go," she said. "I'll see you tomorrow."

As Elizabeth ran up her back steps and into her house, I took a quick look behind me. The alley was empty except for the Parkers' tabby cat prowling around our garbage can. He looked at me and meowed as I latched the gate behind me and dashed inside.

Mother was pushing the vacuum cleaner around the living room. Its roar made it impossible to talk, so I took the dust rag she handed me and flicked it over the radio, the bookcases flanking the mantel, the coffee table, and the matching end tables at either side of the couch.

As much as I hated housework, I was glad to follow Mother from room to room, dusting chair rungs and mirror frames and whatever else needed it. This close to Mother, I was safe from the crazy man.

5

*T*hat evening while Mother and I washed the dishes, I stared out the open kitchen window. The summer dusk was deepening into night, and lightning bugs flickered in the holly trees, but all I could think of was the crazy man. Somewhere in the woods, just across the railroad tracks, he prowled the darkness, knife in hand, looking for a victim.

Bending my head over the glass I was drying, I asked Mother if she'd ever heard any strange rumors about the experimental farm.

She shook her head. "The university tests fertilizers and works on cures for animal diseases," she said. "Things like that. Why?"

"Gordy Smith says a crazy man escaped from there," I told her. "He was an experiment that went wrong or something, and he's hiding in the woods. He has a knife this big." To show her, I held my hands apart the way Gordy had.

Mother laughed. "Why, Margaret, I hope you don't believe that. Those woods aren't big enough for someone to hide in."

"But—" I started to say I'd seen him when I remembered I wasn't allowed to cross the train tracks. If I told Mother any more, she'd know I'd disobeyed a major rule, one she'd insisted on since I learned to walk.

"No buts," Mother said. "Gordy was pulling your leg. Nobody's down in those woods, except maybe an old tramp. Now dry the silverware so we can finish in time to hear 'The Lone Ranger.' "

In the living room, safe beside Mother on the couch, I tried to convince myself I hadn't seen anything in the woods but a trick of shadow and sunlight. Gordy had made me think something was there, that was all. But after the Lone Ranger and his faithful Indian companion rounded up a gang of outlaws and galloped off into the sunset, I stalled for time, begging to stay up longer. When I'd listened to two more shows, Daddy finally lost his patience and ordered me to bed.

Reluctantly, I left the living room and climbed the steps to my room. Pausing in the hall, I glanced at Jimmy's closed door. "If you were home, I wouldn't be scared," I whispered. "You wouldn't let anybody hurt me. You'd take care of me."

But Jimmy wasn't here to keep me safe. It was dark in his room and dark outside, and I was all alone upstairs. With tears pricking at the backs of my eyes, I went into my room and shut the door. Then, as an extra precaution, I shoved a chair against it.

No matter what Elizabeth or Mother said, I'd seen the crazy man. It hadn't been my imagination. He'd been there, just for a second, staring at me. Then he'd disappeared.

*

For the next couple of days, I was very cautious when I left the house. The crazy man might be just ahead, hiding behind a tree or lurking around a corner. He might be sneaking up behind me, he might be lying in wait anywhere in College Hill. To be on the safe side, I stayed away from the train tracks and spent a lot of time looking over my shoulder.

Elizabeth knew what was bothering me, and she teased me for being such a sissy baby. As far as she was concerned, I'd fallen for one of Gordy's stories, a lie he'd made up to keep us away from his hut. It hurt my feelings when she laughed at me and made chicken sounds, but all her teasing couldn't make me disbelieve what I'd seen in the woods.

By the end of the week, I hadn't caught even a glimpse of the crazy man. Not in the daytime. Not in the nighttime, either. I began to think Elizabeth must be right after all. Maybe I'd only seen a harmless old tramp. Maybe nobody was going to get me. Maybe I was safe.

*

One hot afternoon, Elizabeth and I were slouched on the glider on her front porch, drinking ginger ale and looking at *Life*. The big news was the liberation of Paris, and we were poring over pictures of the parade on the Champs-Elysées, searching for Jimmy's face among the hundreds of GIs. I didn't know if he was anywhere near Paris, but I was thinking it would be nice for him to march down the street and get a kiss from a pretty French girl.

While I was imagining the good time Jimmy might be having in Paris, Elizabeth nudged me. "Look, there's Barbara and Brent."

Hearing Elizabeth shout hello, Barbara stopped and waved at us. The sunlight touched her dark hair with red fire as she bent down to smile at the baby in the carriage she was pushing.

Abandoning the magazine, Elizabeth leapt off the top step and ran down the sidewalk, with me at her heels.

As I leaned into the carriage to tickle Brent, I heard our screen door shut. Looking over my shoulder, I saw Mother coming toward us. "I just had to see Brent," she told Barbara.

Pleased to have an audience, Brent cooed and bounced up and down. He was the sort of baby who loved everybody and expected everybody to love him.

"What a darling," Mother said. "How old is he now?"

"Five months today," Barbara said. "He's big for his age, just like his daddy was. Maybe he'll grow up to be a football player, too."

"He reminds me so much of Butch," Mother said. "Especially when he smiles."

Barbara smoothed Brent's hair. "I wish Butch could have seen him. He'd be proud to know he had such a handsome son."

Mother put an arm around Barbara's shoulder and hugged her. "He'd be proud of you, too," she said softly. "You've been a brave girl."

Releasing Barbara, Mother reached into the carriage and scooped up Brent. "Jiggety jiggety jig, to market, to market to buy a fat pig," she sang as she bounced him on her hip.

Brent squealed happily. His rosy face creased into a big smile, and he grabbed Mother's nose.

"You little rascal." Mother laughed and turned to Barbara. "It seems like yesterday Jimmy was this size. I don't know where the time goes. When they're babies, you think they'll never walk or talk or do anything but eat and cry. Then in a minute they're grown up and gone."

"How is Jimmy?" Barbara asked. "Have you heard from him lately?"

"He's all right, I guess," Mother said. "In his last letter he sounded a little blue. I keep hoping he'll be home soon, but the war just drags on and on."

Barbara bit her lip and looked across the street. Mrs. Bedford was hanging sheets out to dry in the backyard, and she waved when she saw us.

Nobody said anything for a few seconds, so I poked my face close to Brent, hoping he'd grab my nose and make us all laugh again. I didn't want to think about Butch going off to war and getting killed in Italy three months after he married Barbara. He'd been my hero, the best quarterback on the high school team. If Butch could die, no one was safe.

Reluctantly, Mother lowered Brent into his carriage. Giving Barbara another big hug, she said, "He's a wonderful baby. You're doing a great job."

Then she looked at me. "Don't you wander off," Mother said. "I'll need some help with dinner in about an hour."

"We're going to walk Barbara home," Elizabeth said. "Is that okay?"

Mother nodded. "Just come straight back. No dillydallying, Margaret." Smiling at Barbara, she said, "Say hi to your folks for me."

Barbara pushed the carriage slowly up Garfield Road, and Elizabeth and I walked along beside her. At the corner, Barbara stopped for a moment to wait for a car to pass. Turning to Elizabeth, she asked, "How's Joe doing?"

"Fine," Elizabeth said. "He can't tell us exactly where he is, but he said his ship hasn't seen much action. Mother says there are worse things than boredom. At least he's not being shot at."

A squeal from Brent interrupted Elizabeth. As she leaned over the carriage to make a silly face, I saw Gordy and Toad trudging toward us, hauling a wagon heaped high with tin cans, hubcaps, and old newspapers and magazines. Doug walked by its side, trying to keep everything from sliding off into the road.

"Wow, look at all the scrap they've collected," Barbara said.

Ignoring Elizabeth and me, Gordy grinned at Barbara. He was wearing his old army helmet, and he was even dirtier than usual. His legs and arms were crisscrossed with briar scratches and scabbed with mosquito bites, and his skin was grimy.

"I bet you never saw anybody get more stuff than this," he said. "Toad and Doug and me know all the best houses."

Elizabeth nudged me. "They probably stole it," she whispered.

"You're really doing your part," Barbara said, and Gordy grinned even more widely.

"Donald's doing his part, too," Gordy boasted. "He's a gunner now, shooting down Nazis." He demonstrated by pointing an imaginary machine gun at the sky and making his usual sound effects.

"How about Stuart?" Barbara asked. "Is he still in basic training, or is he overseas already?"

Gordy hesitated a moment. "Stuart's fine." Turning to

Toad, he said, "Let's get this stuff to my house before we lose it all."

"Well, send your brothers my love," Barbara said, "and tell Stu I miss him."

Gordy didn't answer. Without looking at any of us, he yanked at the wagon, and Doug moved quickly to steady its load.

Barbara watched the boys disappear around a corner. "That poor kid looks so neglected," she said. "When Stu was around, Gordy had somebody to look after him, but now he's got nobody."

"He has his parents, doesn't he?" Elizabeth scowled at Gordy's back. "I sure wouldn't waste my breath worrying about him. Believe you me, Gordy Smith can take care of himself."

"I hope so." Barbara smiled down at Brent. "Let's go home, little fellow," she whispered. "It's almost time for supper."

*

Elizabeth and I walked back from Barbara's house along the trolley tracks. The afternoon sun was still hot, and the steel rails shone like silver. I tried balancing on one, but the metal scorched the soles of my bare feet, and I hopped off. Not Elizabeth. Like a tightrope walker, she strode ahead of me. If she had a mind to, I thought, she could probably walk on hot coals.

When we reached Garfield Road, we left the tracks and turned toward home. "Remember when Barbara and Butch got married?" Elizabeth asked me. "We sat on the curb and watched them come out of Saint Andrew's, and everybody threw rice. Barbara was the most beautiful bride I ever saw."

"And Butch was so handsome."

I walked along silently, thinking about the wedding, feeling sad about Butch, wishing he hadn't died.

"Gordy sure didn't say much about Stuart," Elizabeth said after a while.

"Maybe he hasn't had a chance to shoot down any Nazis yet."

"Maybe not."

We were standing in front of Elizabeth's house, a mirror image of mine. Identical blue stars hung in our living room windows. With all my heart, I hoped neither Elizabeth nor I would ever have gold stars.

"Step on a crack," Elizabeth shouted as she ran up her sidewalk.

"Break Hitler's back!" I yelled, jumping hard on the cement. Then, taking the steps two at a time, I dashed inside just in time to help Mother set the table.

6

*O*n the first day of school, Elizabeth raced up my back steps and pressed her face against the screen door. "Haven't you finished breakfast yet?" she asked me.

I slurped the sugary milk left in my cereal bowl and ran into the bathroom to brush my teeth. Because it was a special occasion, Mother had insisted on rolling my hair up on rags to make it curl, but the humid September weather was already straightening it and it hung way down my back, hot and heavy. Mother should have listened to me and let me wear braids, I thought glumly.

"You look nice," Elizabeth told me as we left the house. "I like your dress."

"Thanks," I said, glad I'd worn my new one. It was dark gray plaid, and it had a round white collar. "I like yours, too."

Elizabeth smiled and smoothed her skirt. Her dress was as blue as her eyes, smocked across the bodice and tied at the back with a sash. Its white collar and cuffs were trimmed with dainty lace. On her feet were brand-new saddle oxfords, spotlessly white and shiny brown, and her socks stood straight up, hugging her legs. Unlike mine, they never slid down.

"How about my shoes?" I scowled at my feet. I'd wanted saddles like Elizabeth's, but all the store had in my size were plain brown oxfords. They looked like army shoes, and, after a summer of going barefoot, they felt stiff and tight.

Elizabeth glanced down and shrugged. "They're not so bad," she said. "Lots of other kids will be wearing them, and they'll hate them just as much as you do."

We walked up Garfield Road and met Polly Anderson on the corner. "Sixth grade at last!" she said. "Now we're number one! Bosses of the whole school!"

"Hooray for us!" Elizabeth shouted.

Judy Katz and Linda Becker yelled when they saw us, and we waited for them at the trolley tracks. Linking arms, we walked up the street together. I was glad to see Polly and Judy were wearing oxfords like mine. Linda had saddles, but hers were black and white, not as pretty as Elizabeth's.

"Are you ready for Mrs. Wagner?" Linda asked me.

"Nobody's ready for her," Elizabeth answered for me. "She's so mean. She yells and makes you stay after school, and if she catches you talking, she sends you out in the hall, just like that!" Elizabeth snapped her fingers.

"And she loads you down with homework," Judy said. "My big sister had her, and she told me I'd better watch out."

"My brother Paul was in her class last year," Polly said. "He got hit lots of times with the ruler. Mrs. Wagner hated him."

"That's nothing new," Elizabeth said. "*Everybody* hates Paul."

I glanced at Polly, but she didn't look the least bit offended by Elizabeth's opinion of her brother. In fact, she nodded her head in agreement.

"There's somebody I hate even worse than Paul." Elizabeth nudged me and pointed across the playground at Gordy slouching along with Doug and Toad.

"The Three Musketeers," Judy said scornfully. "What dopes."

"Come on," Polly said. "The bell's about to ring. I don't want to be late on the first day of school."

As we hurried up the front steps, Gordy ran past me. "The crazy man's coming," he hissed in my ear. "He's going to cut your heart out and eat it for dinner, Magpie."

Startled, I stopped and stared at him, too scared to move. Gordy made a hideous face and leapt at me, waving his arms and gibbering like a monkey.

"Get away from her, you dumbo!" Elizabeth shoved Gordy, but he grabbed her hands.

"Help, help," Gordy yelled, pretending he couldn't escape. "Lizard's throwing herself at me again."

As Elizabeth broke free, Gordy dashed into school and ran to the boys' room. "You can't get me now, Lizard," he said before the door swung shut.

"I despise Gordy Smith," Elizabeth told me. Her face was red and she was breathing hard. "I loathe, abhor, detest, and utterly hate him."

*

It didn't take us long to know why everybody had warned us about Mrs. Wagner. Short and plump, she strode grimly into the classroom and opened her roll book. "Say 'Present' when your name is called," she said. She didn't smile like Miss Carter or speak softly like Mrs. Harper. In fact, when she reached Polly's name, she frowned.

"I hope you're not like your brother," she said.

Passing over me with nothing more than a comment about Jimmy's artistic skills, Mrs. Wagner paused at Elizabeth's name and said, "You'd better be prepared to work hard this year." From the sharp-eyed look she gave her, you could tell she wasn't about to be taken in by big blue eyes and a pretty smile. She must have heard something about Elizabeth and obviously planned to keep an eye on her.

After singling out Gordy, Doug, and Toad for some warnings, she told us to stand for the Pledge of Allegiance and the Lord's Prayer.

When we'd finished, we sat down and folded our hands on our desks while Mrs. Wagner told us her rules.

"There will be no talking unless you are called on," she said. "There will be no note passing. Neatness will count. So will spelling, grammar, and punctuation. Homework will be done on time, and there will be a great deal of it. There will be no tale-telling. I will see everything that goes on in this room, and I will not need the misguided assistance of any child."

As Mrs. Wagner paused to take a breath, I glanced at Gordy. He made a hideous crazy-man face and drew a finger like a knife across his throat. Nervously, I looked at Mrs. Wagner. Had she seen Gordy and me?

"I keep those who misbehave after school," she said. Her eyes lingered on Gordy, before moving on to the rest of the class. "It is not a pleasant experience."

Then, clearing her throat loudly, Mrs. Wagner plunged her hand into the pillowy bosom of her dress, rummaged around, and pulled forth a frilly handkerchief. She then blew her nose so loudly I expected an elephant to stampede through the classroom. No one giggled. Not even Elizabeth.

"I am scrupulously fair," Mrs. Wagner continued. "I have no favorites." Here her eyes lingered on Bonnie Graham, Julie Ryan, and Phyllis Fields, the most stuck-up girls in school and teachers' pets, all three. Only Phyllis blushed. Bonnie and Julie sat and stared at Mrs. Wagner, their faces as hard as stone.

In the silence following her words, Mrs. Wagner handed out our books, and lessons began. Math, spelling, geography, social studies, reading. Mrs. Wagner drilled us as I'd never been drilled before. It was going to be a long, hard year.

*

At three-thirty, we raced across the playground, glad to be free. As soon as we were out of sight of the school, Elizabeth pretended to pull a handkerchief out of her dress. After groping around in an exaggerated imitation of Mrs. Wagner, she made a loud trumpeting sound.

"I have no favorites," she proclaimed. "I hate all of you *exactly* the same, and I will be scrupulously unfair to each and every one of you. I keep those who misbehave in a special dungeon under the school. You will be chained to the wall and fed bread and water. Some of you will be shot at dawn. It will not be a pleasant experience, but I hope to give it to all of you, especially Elizabeth, Polly, Gordy, Doug, and Toad."

We all laughed, but I swore to myself I would do my homework, even math, and be very careful with my commas and periods, as well as my spelling. This year I would not read library books in my lap when I was supposed to be doing geography, I would pay attention instead of day-dreaming, I would draw only when we were having art, I would talk only when I was called on, and I would never tell tales on anyone. No matter what I saw, I would keep my mouth shut and stay in Mrs. Wagner's good graces.

7

One October morning Elizabeth and I were walking to school. While she kicked her way through neatly raked heaps of fallen leaves, scattering them in all directions, I plodded along behind her, trying to read my arithmetic book and walk at the same time without tripping over something. Mrs. Wagner had just begun a unit on decimals, and I still hadn't figured out our homework assignment.

It didn't help that Elizabeth was singing, "from the halls of Montezuma to the shores of Tripoli" at the top of her lungs as she torpedoed leaf pile after leaf pile. How could I concentrate on decimals with all the noise she was making?

Suddenly she stopped singing and grabbed my arm. "Oh, no," she said. "Not him. My day is ruined."

I raised my eyes from my arithmetic book. Two blocks ahead, Bruce Benson, our patrol boy, was herding a bunch of little kids across the street, but between him and us was Gordy. Slumped against a telephone pole, his hands jammed in the pockets of his old knickers, he was kicking at the ground and scowling. Even from this distance, he looked meaner, madder, and uglier than usual.

"Come on," I said, grabbing Elizabeth's hand, "we can go to school another way." I tugged at her, anxious to escape before Gordy spotted us.

Refusing to budge, Elizabeth pulled her hand away. "Don't be such a scaredy-cat, Margaret."

"Quick," I said, trying to drag her up the trolley tracks. "He's going to notice us any minute."

"So what?" Elizabeth tossed her head. "There's two of us, and only one of him. What can he do?"

Plenty, I thought, but Elizabeth was walking straight toward Gordy, swinging her bookbag, her nose wrinkled as if she smelled a disgusting odor.

Trotting along behind Elizabeth, I tried to ignore Gordy, but it wasn't easy when he yelled, "Hey, Lizard and Baby Magpie, you better watch out."

Stepping in front of us, Gordy blocked the sidewalk, daring us to walk around him.

"The crazy man's looking for you," he said.

"Get out of the way," Elizabeth said. "I'm not scared of you or your dumb old crazy man."

"He's got his knife all sharpened up, so he can cut your hearts out. He likes to eat them raw, dripping with blood." Gordy made a hideous slurping sound.

Scared as I was, I sneaked a quick glance at him. One of his eyes was swollen shut, and the skin was purple and red and blue around it. It made my face hurt to look at it, and I turned my head away.

"Who gave you that shiner?" Elizabeth asked. "Your little sister?"

"Shut up, Lizard." Gordy shoved Elizabeth so hard she staggered backward and fell.

When she got to her feet, her knee was bleeding. I watched the blood trickle down her shin and stain her white sock.

Furious, Elizabeth slung her book bag at Gordy, but he

grabbed it and yanked it away from her. Before she could stop him, he pulled her notebook out. While she struggled to get it back, he tore her homework to bits. Little fragments of Elizabeth's neat handwriting fell on the sidewalk. Then he opened her brand-new box of Crayolas, the big one she'd just bought, and tossed the crayons everywhere.

"Stop it! Stop!" she cried as Gordy scattered the rest of her things. Pencils, a ruler, an unused art gum eraser, her fountain pen, her bottle of blue ink—all flew into the air and rolled into the grass, into the gutter, out into the street.

Screaming for Bruce, I tried to rescue Elizabeth's things without losing mine. Finally Bruce and Frankie, the patrol from Beech Drive, came running toward us.

"Quit it, Gordy," Bruce yelled. "Leave her alone!"

Gordy tossed Elizabeth's empty book bag at her. Deliberately stepping on as many crayons as he could, he sauntered toward school. "Report me to Wagner, Benson," he called back, "and see what happens to you."

Silently, the four of us gathered Elizabeth's school supplies. Her crayons were ruined, but we poked them back into the box anyway. Her pen and ink were all right, and, except for their broken points, so were her pencils. Gordy had torn most of her notebook paper, and the homework was beyond hope.

Her face flushed, her hair hiding her eyes, Elizabeth dumped everything into her bookbag. Slinging its strap over her shoulder, she started walking toward school. One tear trembled on the rim of her eye. When she blinked, it slid slowly down her cheek. Quickly, she wiped it away with the back of her hand. Elizabeth Crawford did not cry.

"Well," she said, "are you going to tell Mrs. Wagner what he did?"

Bruce's face turned red, and Frankie kicked a stone.

"He'll just deny it," Bruce said. His curly blonde hair fluffed up in the humid air, and he wiped some perspiration from his forehead with his shirtsleeve.

"But four people saw him," Elizabeth said.

"I know, but . . ." Bruce toyed with the little silver badge on his patrol belt.

"You don't deserve to wear that!" Elizabeth said. "You sissy baby, you're scared of Gordy."

"Mrs. Wagner said we shouldn't tell on each other," Frankie said. "Didn't she say that?" he asked Bruce when Elizabeth glared at him.

Bruce nodded. We were at the bottom of the steps now, and Gordy was standing at the top, grinning down at us. Doug and Toad had appeared from somewhere, and they flanked Gordy like a pair of bodyguards.

"We'll get you if you tell," Gordy said to Bruce. "Wherever you hide, we'll find you."

Elizabeth clenched her fists and glared at Gordy. Then she turned to Bruce. "So that's it?" she said. "He ruins my school supplies and tears up my homework, and you don't do anything?"

A group of kids ran past us. "Hurry up, the bell's about to ring," one shouted.

Her back rigid with anger, Elizabeth climbed the steps. Gordy lounged in the doorway, waiting for her, and she had to squeeze past him to go inside.

"Hey, Lizard," he whispered. "If you tell, I'll give your address to the crazy man. Me and him are buddies now."

"You just wait, Gordy Smith," Elizabeth said. "Bruce

and Frankie might be scared of you, but I'm not. I'll get you for this, I swear I will."

I was so close to Elizabeth I was practically stepping on her heels, but Gordy grabbed one of my braids and stared right into my eyes. "The crazy man told me he's going to kill you first, Magpie."

Too frightened to speak, I pulled away from him and followed Elizabeth into our classroom. The whole time Mrs. Wagner called roll, I felt Gordy's eyes boring into me, daring me to tell. He had nothing to worry about. I wasn't about to tattle.

*

By the time school was out, Elizabeth was so mad she was sizzling. Not only had Bruce refused to report Gordy, but Mrs. Wagner had made Elizabeth stay in at recess and do her homework over again.

As we walked home, Elizabeth stamped the sidewalk. "Step on a crack, break *Gordy's* back!" she yelled each time she put her foot down.

Polly and I joined in. Instead of Hitler's face, I pictured Gordy's face under my big, shiny army shoes—his pale skin, his freckles, the scar over his eyebrow, his black eye. As I stamped harder and harder on his image, my heart filled with rage. I hated him almost as much as I hated Hitler.

We waved good-bye to Polly at the corner and walked on down Garfield. Elizabeth was calmer now and very quiet. Too quiet, I thought.

In front of her house, Elizabeth stopped and stared at me. "We're going to make Gordy sorry for all the things he's done to us," she said.

My mouth went dry as she told me what she planned to do. "Every Saturday morning, Gordy, Toad, and Doug play football," she said. "While they're doing that, we'll wreck their hut. It'll be our D day."

"What about the crazy man?" I asked. I was getting weak in the knees just thinking about going down in the woods again.

Elizabeth frowned. "How often do I have to tell you? Gordy made him up to scare us. There isn't a crazy man!"

"I'm not going there." My voice was rising into a whine, but I didn't care.

Elizabeth tossed her curls. "Well, I guess I'll have to go by myself, Baby Magpie," she said. "You aren't my friend after all, are you? I can't count on you for anything."

Tilting her chin up, she turned and walked away. When she reached her top step, she paused and looked back at me. "You yellow coward sissy baby," she said and went inside, slamming the door behind her.

For a moment, her words hung in the silent air. I was sure everyone in the neighborhood must have heard them.

Ashamed of my cowardice, I ran up Elizabeth's sidewalk. "Okay, okay," I yelled at her house. "I'll go!"

Opening the door, Elizabeth grinned at me. "That's more like it," she said. "We'll fix Gordy good, we really will, Margaret. And if we see the crazy man, I'll protect you."

8

*O*n Saturday morning, I was lying on my bed listening to "Let's Pretend," my favorite show. Uncle Bill had just whisked the children away on their flying carpet when Elizabeth arrived. Without a word, she turned off the radio.

"Let's pretend you're as brave as I am," she said.

Reluctantly, I followed her downstairs. Mother was sitting at the kitchen table drinking a cup of tea and listening to the radio.

"Elizabeth and I are going outside to play for a while," I told her. As much as I hated chores, I lingered by the door for a moment, praying Mother would tell me I couldn't go anywhere till I vacuumed the living room. But she just smiled.

"Have a nice time," she said, "but be back in time for lunch."

I felt like telling her she might never see me again, at least not in one piece, but Elizabeth grabbed my hand and yanked me through the door as if she could see into the depths of my cowardly heart. Nothing was going to stop her from getting her revenge on Gordy. Not Gordy himself, not me or Mother, not even the crazy man roaming the woods with his big, sharp knife.

We ran down the alley and paused on the railroad bank

to see if anyone was in sight. All we saw was Mr. Zimmerman walking his dog. As he vanished around the corner without giving us a second look, we dashed across the train tracks.

In the field, the goldenrod was in full bloom, and the leaves of the sumac were edged with crimson. The woods flamed red and gold and green under the blue sky. Just looking at the silent trees filled me with dread.

"Pretend we're soldiers on patrol," Elizabeth whispered as she climbed over the fence. "The hut is a Nazi outpost."

Fearfully, I crept through the bushes behind Elizabeth. Like a jungle, the foliage closed in around us, so dense the crazy man could be a few feet away, watching us, biding his time, his knife ready. Here and there, wild grape vines hung like tangled ropes, and things rustled and shook and whispered in the leaves.

"We're close now," Elizabeth said. "I remember that tree."

She pointed at a huge oak with a hole in its trunk, and, a few seconds later, we saw the hut. Like soldiers, we watched it silently for a while, but we heard nothing. It seemed empty, an old shack abandoned by its owners and listing slightly to one side.

Elizabeth reached into the pocket of her overalls and pulled out a handful of broken crayons, Gordy's handiwork. "What we'll do is write stuff on the walls," she whispered, "like 'Kilroy was here' and cuss words."

"I thought we were going to tear it down."

Elizabeth bit her lip and frowned. "I don't think we can," she said. "It's built too good. We'll just mess it up. Steal their stuff and all."

"Couldn't we just write on the *outside?*" I was following

her across the clearing now, wincing every time a twig snapped under my feet.

Elizabeth gave me one of her most scornful looks. "You are such a coward," she said.

"But if we're inside we might not hear them coming," I said. "We'll be trapped."

"That's true," Elizabeth said. "You stay outside and stand guard. If you see anybody, yell, and we'll run."

She thrust a black crayon at me. "Start writing," she said and then pushed the door open slowly.

I watched her go inside, and then I scrawled "Kilroy was here" in big letters on the wall. It took me a while because I kept looking over my shoulder, fearful of every noise. At any moment I expected the crazy man to lunge out of the trees, his knife raised.

"Margaret," Elizabeth called, "come in here. You've got to see this!"

Scanning the woods first and seeing nothing, I slipped through the doorway. Despite two windows, the hut was dark inside. It smelled of moldy leaves and damp earth, and I shivered.

"There's blankets and a railroad lantern and food, books, all kinds of stuff," Elizabeth said. "You'd think somebody lived here."

As my eyes grew accustomed to the dim light, I saw what Elizabeth meant. A bookcase made from an orange crate held magazines and a few tattered books. Another orange crate was full of canned food. The lantern sat on the dirt floor by a pile of blankets. Pinup girls plastered the walls. Every one of them had been given a beard and a mustache and a few blackened teeth.

54

There was also a knife. A big one. Just like the knife Gordy said the crazy man carried.

"Let's get out of here," I whispered. "Fast."

But Elizabeth was shoving things, tossing books around, tearing pages out of magazines, wrecking the place. "Wa-hoo!" she yelled as she grabbed a can of Campbell's Soup and hurled it through the window. "Yi-yi-yi!"

The sound of the breaking glass and the sight of Elizabeth's flushed face excited me. Forgetting my fears, I snatched up the knife and slashed at the pinups. Then I gathered the cans of food and threw them. As the glass broke, I shrieked like an Indian on the warpath.

When there was nothing left to destroy, we ran outside, still whooping and hollering.

"We did it, we did it," Elizabeth cried. "After this, they won't ever think we're just dumb girls! Not us!"

We ran through the woods toward home, and a gust of wind came after us, pummeling us, pushing us, making me feel as giddy as the branches swaying over my head.

"Wa-hoo!" Elizabeth screamed again. "Yi-yi-yi!"

"Wa-hoo!" I echoed. With a burst of energy, I raced past her. I was running faster than she was, faster than I'd ever run, faster than the wind itself. At any moment, I would fly up into the air and soar away. Now, like Elizabeth, I was Wonder Woman, Superwoman, Mary Marvel, powerful, invincible, undefeatable.

"Wa-hoo!" I shrieked again and glanced back at Elizabeth.

That was when I saw him. For a second, I stopped, frozen in flight, my heart pounding like a rabbit's. For a long and terrible moment we stared at each other through a tangle of grapevines and poison ivy.

"Run!" I screamed at Elizabeth. "It's him, the crazy man, he's coming after us!"

Elizabeth looked over her shoulder, saw what I saw, and gasped. Expecting to feel the man's knife pierce our hearts, the two of us dashed through the woods, leapt the fence, and tore across the field toward the safety of the train tracks, the back alley, and home.

9

*B*y the time we reached my back gate, I thought my heart was going to burst right out of my chest. Safe in the yard, we crawled into the clump of lilac bushes we'd used as our hideout when we were too little to cross the street without an adult. Trembling and gasping for breath, we crouched on the damp earth and stared at each other.

When Elizabeth could speak, she said, "Gordy wasn't lying, and neither were you. You really did see him." Her voice shook, but she got to her knees and peered through the branches. The alley was empty and silent.

"He'll wait till dark," I croaked. "Then he'll come and murder us in our beds."

"Don't say that!" Elizabeth grabbed my shoulders so tightly she made my bones ache. Her face was inches from mine, and her breath was warm on my cheeks. "He doesn't know where we live or who we are."

"He'll find us. You heard what Gordy said, he'll give him our address," I sobbed. Like the Shadow, the crazy man would creep into our house, invisible to Mother and Daddy. The stairs would creak under his feet, and he would pause outside my closed door and laugh softly before entering.

"He won't come, Margaret, he won't!" For once, Elizabeth looked as scared as I felt.

Pushing her away, I sat on the ground and cried. No matter what she said, Elizabeth couldn't convince me we were safe. All my life I had expected something to get me. When I was little, it had been the long-armed witch under the bed, the wolf behind the door, the monster in the closet. Now it was the crazy man. Only Jimmy could save me, but he wasn't here and there was no escape.

"Elizabeth! Elizabeth!" Mrs. Crawford called from her back porch. "Lunchtime!"

Giving me a shove, Elizabeth said, "Stop bawling, Margaret, stop it! What will your mother think if she sees you crying like a baby? You can't tell what we did, you can't!"

"Elizabeth Crawford!" Mrs. Crawford yelled, louder this time. "I'm about to start counting, young lady."

"Coming!" Elizabeth shouted and made a face her mother couldn't see. "I'm serious, Margaret. Don't tell!"

"One, two, three," Mrs. Crawford began. If she reached ten before Elizabeth got home, Mrs. Crawford would spank her.

Elizabeth made another face, worse than the first. Then she stood up and brushed the dirt and leaves off her overalls. "He's not coming," she said before she ran home.

Just as Mrs. Crawford yelled, "Ten!" Elizabeth charged through her kitchen door. I could hear the whack she got on her fanny as I darted up my back porch steps.

"You're just in time for soup and a sandwich," Mother said. When she turned around and saw my face, though, she almost dropped the spoon she'd been using to stir the soup.

"Margaret, what's wrong?" she asked. "You look like you've seen a ghost."

I slung my arms around her and hugged her hard, pressing my face against her soft bosom, feeling safe in the warm kitchen.

"Did you have a fight with Elizabeth?" Mother asked. Whenever I came home in tears, she always blamed it on Elizabeth. Often she was right, but not this time. We hadn't had a bad fight for ages. Our war with Gordy had given Elizabeth a real enemy.

I shook my head, but Mother wasn't convinced. "Did she say something that hurt your feelings?"

"No," I said. "No."

"You've got to stand up for yourself, Margaret," Mother went on as if she were deaf. "You can't let that child push you around. She's not the only girl in the world, you know. Just because she lives next door doesn't mean you have to spend all your time with her. You could play with Julie Ryan or Phyllis Fields—nice girls who don't go around acting like smart alecks all the time."

"Elizabeth didn't do anything!" I yelled. "She's my best friend! Julie and Phyllis hate me, and I hate them!"

Mother frowned. "I don't like that tone of voice," she said. "That's Elizabeth I hear, not you."

She put my soup and sandwich on the kitchen table and stood back, her arms folded. "Go wash your hands and face," she said. "Then sit down and eat your lunch."

*

After dinner that evening, Elizabeth came over and we sat on the front steps, sharing a cherry Popsicle. Inside, Daddy and Mother were listening to the war news. Except for the radio, the only sound was the cheep, cheep, cheep of crickets under the porch. Even though it was October,

59

the night was as warm as summer. A full moon hovered over the roof of the Bedfords' house, silvering the shingles, but somewhere in the darkness a maniac lurked, waiting for an opportunity to seize me.

"Where do you think he is right now?" I asked Elizabeth.

"Who?" In the light pouring out of the living room windows behind her, her hair glowed but her face was a dim oval as she leaned toward me.

"The crazy man."

We both looked down the street. The row of holly trees near our house hid the train tracks and the dark woods beyond them, but a person could be crouching there, in my yard, watching us at this very moment. Nervously, I sucked the last bit of Popsicle from the stick and chewed on the wood.

Elizabeth pushed her hair out of her eyes. "I've been thinking about him," she said. "Maybe we just saw some old hobo who jumped off a freight train. My father says plenty of them still come through here, and he should know. He's had to go down in the woods and arrest them lots of times."

"You told your father where we were today?"

"Are you nuts?" Elizabeth stared at me. "Would I be sitting here if he knew I crossed the train tracks? I'd be locked in my room for the rest of my life."

She snapped her Popsicle stick in half and tossed the pieces into the ivy beside the steps. "I just asked him if he'd ever heard of any dangerous escaped crazy men loose in the woods."

"What did he say?"

"He laughed, Margaret. I felt like a real dumbo."

"I asked Mother about it the first time I saw him, and she laughed too," I admitted. "She said Gordy was just pulling my leg."

"What did I tell you? He made him up to keep us away from his hut, that's all. Whoever we saw in the woods wasn't any crazy man. He was just some old bum."

I chewed harder on my Popsicle stick and stared at the dark row of holly trees. Part of me knew Elizabeth was right, but another part of me was sure the crazy man was hiding in the shadows. I could imagine the moonlight shining on his knife and the sly smile on his face as he listened to Elizabeth prattle about harmless hoboes. Oh, he'd show us, he was thinking, yes indeed he would.

*

That night I lay in bed with the cover pulled up to my chin, hugging my teddy bear, scared to close my eyes. Why had I gone into the woods with Elizabeth? Why had I helped her wreck the hut? With shame, I remembered the wild excitement of smashing things. I saw Elizabeth's flushed face, I heard her whooping as she tore up a magazine and broke the window. If only I'd stayed home and listened to "Let's Pretend."

Unable to sleep, I turned on my light. I didn't care if Mother saw it or not. I wasn't going to lie alone in the dark, waiting for the crazy man to come and kill me.

Downstairs I heard my parents getting ready for bed. On Saturday nights they always listened to "Your Hit Parade" and then sat around talking or reading for a while. Now it was past eleven. In a little while they would be asleep, and the crazy man would know it was safe to crawl through a window and sneak upstairs to my room.

"Margaret," Mother called up the steps, "is your light still on?"

When I didn't say anything, she came to see why. Her footsteps were brisk and determined. Poking her head into my room, she stared at me. "Why aren't you asleep? Did you have a nightmare?"

She sat down on the edge of my bed, and I threw my arms around her. I wanted to beg her to lie down and sleep beside me all night, but I was afraid a request like that would make her angry. What a baby she would think I was.

"There, there," Mother said, stroking my hair as if I were still a little girl, "it was just a dream. Don't be so silly."

"Can't I keep my light on?" I sobbed. "Just tonight?"

She shook her head. "Do you know what my mother used to do when I was scared to go to sleep?" Mother picked up my oxfords. She held them toward me so that one shoe pointed ahead, the other behind. "She'd put them by my bed like this." She set them on the floor. "Now no evil spirit can come near you."

"Why not? What stops it?"

"It gets confused, I guess, and doesn't know which way to go." Mother shrugged and gave me a little hug. "Anyway, that's what my mother told me and what her mother told her. It must be true because I'm sitting here telling you about it. What more proof do you need?"

Mother smiled then and switched off the light. "It even worked for Jimmy," she added.

"Jimmy was scared of the dark?" I stared at her, sure she was kidding me.

Mother laughed. "When he was little, he was worse than you. Your father said it was just a trick to put off going to sleep. You know, like asking for another drink of water. But he had a real imagination, your brother did. For years he lined his shoes up like that."

Blowing me a kiss from the doorway, Mother said, "No more nonsense now, Margaret. I don't want to hear another peep out of you."

I lay still and listened to Mother go downstairs. When the house was quiet, I leaned over the edge of my bed to make sure my shoes still pointed in opposite directions. Feeling safer, I hugged my bear for a little extra protection and snuggled down under the covers.

Before I fell asleep, I wondered if Jimmy still believed in the shoe trick. In my next letter, I'd try to remember to ask him.

10

*A*lthough I was still afraid of the crazy man, Elizabeth did her best to convince me that Gordy was our only worry. She was sure he'd guessed we were the ones who vandalized his hut. From the way he scowled at us across the classroom, I think she was right.

To protect ourselves, we walked to and from school with Polly, Linda, and Judy. We played jump rope and jacks at recess instead of joining the boys' kickball games, and we stayed in our own yards instead of riding Joe's bike or roller skating.

Eventually, though, we got careless. One afternoon we went to Polly's house. Her older sister had a Victrola and a big stack of records, and we stayed a long time, taking jitterbug lessons from Jean. It was almost five o'clock when we left, and our shadows stretched ahead of us, long and skinny. Elizabeth was singing "Boogie Woogie Bugle Boy" and practicing some of the fancy steps Jean had taught us.

"Like this, see?" she said, twirling around. She was worried I was never going to learn to dance. "It's easy, Margaret."

But, as Mother said, I was born with two left feet and no rhythm at all. In my soul I could feel the beat of the dance music, but I couldn't get the message through to my big old army shoes.

Elizabeth stopped. With her hands on her hips, she watched me. "You're just not trying," she said.

Suddenly a third shadow jutted out in front of us. We whirled around, but it was too late. Gordy grabbed Elizabeth and shook her like a rat.

"Don't you ever go near my hut again," he yelled at her. "I'll kill you, Lizard, I swear I will, if you touch one thing that belongs to me."

"I never went near your dumb old hut!" Elizabeth shouted. Her face was red with anger as she struggled to get away. "It was the crazy man. He did it. Margaret and me saw him. He went inside and busted up everything!"

Gordy started cursing. Grabbing a fistful of her hair, he pulled so hard Elizabeth's head jerked sideways. When she screamed, he let go, but strands of white-blonde hair clung to his hands like spiderwebs.

"Don't say nothing about the crazy man," he said. "I'll cut your heart out myself if you tell a single living soul about him."

I don't know what would have happened if Barbara hadn't come around the corner just then. She was pushing Brent's carriage, and when she saw us she smiled and waved.

Breaking away from Gordy, Elizabeth and I raced toward her. In a moment, we were safe. As Elizabeth bent over the carriage to kiss Brent, I looked back. For a second, Gordy and I stared at each other. Then he spat in the dirt and walked away.

*

For several weeks after that, Gordy didn't bother us. October flowed into November. The weather turned much colder just after Thanksgiving, and at about the same time the war got worse. All the hope we'd had during the summer waned. Butter, sugar, coffee, and gasoline were harder and harder to find. Every day the *Evening Star* was black with scary headlines, and more gold stars appeared in windows. It seemed like the war was going to last forever.

One afternoon in December, Elizabeth and I were sitting in our tree. The sky was blue, but the wind took all the warmth from the sunlight. I had on a pair of Jimmy's old corduroy overalls and the wool warm-up jacket he'd worn in high school. The jacket was way too big for me, but it kept me warm, and I loved the Hyattsdale Hawk embroidered on the back.

"You know what?" Elizabeth asked. "We look like boys." She glanced down at Joe's old pea coat. On her feet were a ragged pair of his black high-top basketball shoes.

In all honesty, I didn't think anyone would ever mistake Elizabeth for a boy. She was just too pretty. A tall, gangly kid like me was another story. Unobservant strangers had called me "Sonny" more than once.

"When the war's over, the first thing I'm getting is a new coat," Elizabeth said. "I saw just the one I want in the Sears catalog. It's blue, and it has a big fur collar. It's so pretty."

"I'm getting saddle oxfords," I said, "and roller skates. Maybe even a bike of my own."

"And all the candy we can eat," Elizabeth went on.

"And no more Spam," I added.

Elizabeth pulled a pack of gum out of her pocket and offered me a stick. Popping it into my mouth, I chewed silently. Big white clouds floated by over our heads. They looked like angels with spread wings, I thought, hovering above us, protecting us.

"Look," Elizabeth said.

Way down the train tracks, Gordy and Doug were crossing the rails. They each carried a bulging grocery bag. We watched them vanish into the woods.

"They must be going to their stupid old hut," Elizabeth said. "Have you ever wondered why they aren't scared of the so-called crazy man?"

I stared at Elizabeth uneasily. "He hates girls," I said, "and they're boys. They don't have anything to worry about."

Elizabeth chewed her gum quietly for a while. "Suppose he's a Nazi spy?" she asked me suddenly.

"Who?"

"The crazy man, dumbo." Elizabeth leaned toward me. "Maybe Gordy tells him things."

"Like what?"

"Government secrets."

"How would Gordy know any secrets?"

Instead of answering, Elizabeth grabbed a limb and swung down from the tree.

"Where are you going?" I called after her.

"Following them," she yelled.

Darting across the tracks, Elizabeth looked back and signaled me to hurry. On fear-trembly legs, I scrambled over the fence and sneaked through the woods after her. We ran from tree to tree, pausing frequently to look and listen. Over our heads, the wind sighed in the bare branches, and the leaves were ankle deep on the ground.

Occasionally a crow or a blue jay cried. The boys were nowhere in sight.

When we neared the hut, we crouched behind a tree and stared at the smoke rising from the crooked chimney. The holes Elizabeth and I had smashed in the windows were covered with cardboard, and someone had scrubbed "Kilroy was here" off the walls.

"I bet a Nazi is in there with them right this minute," Elizabeth whispered.

Nazi or crazy man, I didn't want to meet him. Squatting beside Elizabeth, I looked over my shoulder. All I saw behind me were bare trees and tangles of leafless shrubbery and vines. Stripped of foliage, the woods were bleak and open. Anyone could see us from a long way off, and I wanted to sneak away.

Nervously, I nudged Elizabeth, but, before I could speak, the door of the hut suddenly opened, and the crazy man stepped outside. At the sight of him, my heart pounded so hard I was sure he'd hear it, but he walked off into the woods. He stopped near a tree, and, when I realized what he was doing, I shut my eyes.

After the noise of falling water stopped, I heard the man crunching back over the leaves toward the hut. I opened my eyes then and got my first good look at him. He had a bushy beard and shaggy dark hair, but he was young, maybe about Jimmy's age or even younger. He was wearing army clothes, the kind soldiers wear in battle, but they hung on his skinny body like they belonged to someone else, someone much bigger.

While I watched, Gordy and Doug joined the man. He lit a cigarette and handed Gordy the pack. For a few minutes, nobody said anything. They just sat on a log smoking.

"You're awful thin," Gordy said after a while. "Are you sure you're getting enough to eat?"

The man smiled. "It's probably more than I'd be getting over there."

While Elizabeth and I crouched motionless behind the tree, Gordy, Doug, and the man finished their cigarettes.

"When's it going to be over?" the man asked. His voice was soft and sad. He sounded tired.

"Beats me." Gordy shook his head. He had on a scuffed-up leather jacket and a matching helmet like bomber pilots wear. The chin strap was unbuckled, and the wind clinked the metal parts every now and then. "The news gets worse every day."

"Let's go inside," Doug said. "No sense freezing our tails out here."

The man nodded, and I watched them go into the hut and shut the door.

As soon as it was safe to move, Elizabeth whispered, "Let's go."

With the wind moaning over our heads, we crept away from the hut. When we were out of the boys' hearing, we ran through the woods, ducking branches and dodging the long arms of bramble bushes, not caring how much noise we made. All we wanted to do was get back to our side of the train tracks.

Neither of us said a word until we were in our alley. Then Elizabeth turned to me, her cheeks and nose red from the wind. "Oh, my lord," she whispered, "I know who he is."

I stared at her, but she teased me with her secret for a few seconds.

"He's not crazy and he's not an old bum and he's not a Nazi," she said finally. "He's a dirty, rotten, low-down coward."

"What do you mean?" I stared at her.

"Didn't you recognize him?"

I bit my lip and thought hard. There had been something familiar about the man, but I couldn't think who he reminded me of.

"It was Gordy's brother Stuart," Elizabeth said. "Gordy must be helping him hide from the army."

"Golly, you're right," I whispered. "It *was* Stuart. He's so skinny I didn't even recognize him!"

Elizabeth whistled. "That's why Gordy never brags about Stuart. He's a deserter, Margaret!"

"I'm going to tell Daddy," I said, breaking into a run. "That's against the law!"

"No, wait!" Elizabeth grabbed my arm and yanked me back. "Don't you see? We've got something on Gordy now. He'll do anything to keep us from blabbing about Stuart."

"But it's not fair, Elizabeth. If our brothers went to war, Stuart has to go, too."

With the toe of my sneaker, I scuffed at the cinders packed into the alley's ruts. The wind tweaked at my neck and nipped my nose. At my back were the train tracks and the woods and the deserter. Not a crazy man to keep me awake all night, not a Nazi spy to help Germany defeat us, but Gordy's brother Stuart. A yellow-livered skunk, a man too low to fight for his country.

"We can tell later," Elizabeth said. "But not yet. First let's make Gordy pay for all he's done to us."

I bit my lip and tried to back away, but she had me by the shoulders, forcing me to stay close.

"Come on, Margaret," Elizabeth said, "don't ruin our only chance to get even."

"Okay, okay," I muttered.

Elizabeth hooked her little finger with mine to make my promise official and then ran home.

Ducking under the half-frozen sheets and towels hanging on the clothesline, I crossed the lawn and trudged up my back steps. Alone in my room, I sat down at my desk and spread out my homework. Social studies, long division, spelling words—how did Mrs. Wagner expect us to do all this in just one weekend? I felt tired just looking at it.

Instead of getting to work, I doodled on a piece of notebook paper and tried to remember all I knew about Stuart.

He'd been our paperboy for a while, probably just before he graduated from high school. I had a memory of my parents sitting on the porch one afternoon. Daddy was holding the *Evening Star* Stuart had just delivered and watching him go on down the street, lugging his sack of newspapers. "That's the only Smith who'll ever amount to anything," Daddy had said.

It must have been just after Donald Smith blew up the toilet at the Esso station with a firecracker. Or maybe Daddy was thinking of the night Donald wrecked a trolley car by putting a garbage can on the tracks. Donald did so many awful things it was hard to say. But now he was a gunner, shooting down Nazi planes, doing his part for America. And what was Stuart doing?

Thinking harder, I dragged up a recollection of Stuart watching Jimmy, Joe Crawford, Butch Thompson, and Harold Bedford play basketball behind our garage. He didn't play himself, probably because he was younger than the others, but he seemed to enjoy being there. He was skinny even then, and his clothes never fit him right. His pants were always either too long or too short, his shirts didn't stay tucked in, and he never had a warm coat. On the coldest days, he wore a thin sweater.

I guess in some ways Stuart was kind of pitiful, and some of the boys teased him. For instance, Joe Crawford thought Stuart was a sissy because Donald always made him cry when they were little. Even in high school Joe remembered that and wouldn't let Stuart forget it.

But Jimmy always took up for Stuart. He called him the little poet because he always had his nose in a book. Now that I thought about it, I realized Jimmy liked Stuart.

What would he think if he knew what I knew? Surely Jimmy would agree it was wrong for Stuart to hide in the woods. It was bad to be a deserter, everyone knew that, but I had a feeling Jimmy wouldn't hate him for it. He wouldn't want me to blab either. "Not the little poet, Maggie May," Jimmy would say. "You can't tell on the little poet."

I stared out the window at the bare branches of the maple tree, so black against the red sunset. On my notebook paper I'd doodled a picture of a princess, like the ones Jimmy used to draw for me.

Suppose my brother was down there in that hut? How

would I feel if someone turned him in? I sighed and put my head on my desk. If I hadn't followed Elizabeth across the train tracks, if I hadn't spied on Gordy, I wouldn't know about Stuart, and I wouldn't have to ask myself questions I couldn't answer.

11

*T*he next week, Mrs. Wagner kept us busy, but the following Saturday Elizabeth burst into my room and thrust a sheet of paper at me. "Read this and tell me what you think," she said.

In scrawling penmanship, Elizabeth had written:

> *Dear Gordy,*
>   *We know you are hiding a dirty coward deserter in your hut. We also know who he is—your yellow brother Stuart. Maybe we will tell, maybe we won't. That's for us to know and you to find out!*
>   *Suspensefully yours,*
>   *Two Anonamus Enemies*
> *P.S. You stink.*

"Well, what do you think?" Elizabeth perched on the foot of the bed, grinning. "Didn't I do a good job of disguising my handwriting? I bet even Mrs. Wagner wouldn't recognize it."

It did indeed look amazingly sloppy, large and loopy and slanting backward instead of forward.

"I wrote with my left hand," Elizabeth confessed. "I was going to write more, but it took so long, I got tired of it."

"You spelled 'anonymous' wrong," I told her.

Elizabeth shrugged. "Who cares? I'm not getting a grade on it."

"If we don't sign our names, how can we blackmail Gordy into being nice?" I asked.

"Oh, this is just the first letter," Elizabeth said. "We'll let him worry for a week, then we'll reveal our true identities."

Though I didn't dare say it, I though Elizabeth had been listening to too many radio shows. She sounded like one of the Shadow's enemies. Looking at her sprawled on my bed, rereading her letter, it occurred to me she was the first girl I'd ever known who might grow up to be a criminal.

*

After lunch, Elizabeth and I set out to deliver Gordy's letter. I wanted to send it through the regular mail. I even offered to pay for the stamp, but Elizabeth insisted on hand carrying it to his house.

"What if he sees us?" I asked her as we crept along behind the sagging fence bordering Gordy's yard.

"He won't," she said with a lot more confidence than I felt.

"How about his father?" I asked. In some ways, I was more scared of Mr. Smith than I was of Gordy.

"Quit worrying, Margaret," Elizabeth said. "I know what I'm doing."

Crouching even lower, she peered through the fence at Gordy's house. At first glance, it seemed almost identical to the shingled bungalows on Garfield Road, but, unlike them, its paint was worn to a dingy gray. The front door was scuffed and scarred. An old refrigerator stood on the porch, and one of the windows was covered with cardboard.

In the yard, a broken swing dangled from a tree, and a couple of tricycles and a scooter lay on their sides in the dirt. I saw Gordy's wagon, but I didn't see his bicycle.

"Do you think he's home?" I whispered.

Elizabeth shook her head. "Let's watch the house for a while to make sure."

We squatted for so long my knees ached, but nothing happened. No one came, no one left. A thin stream of smoke rose from the chimney and drifted away on the wind. The swing's rope twisted and untwisted, and its broken seat clacked against the tree trunk. The longer I stared at the dark windows, at the paint peeling away from the sills, at the naked baby doll lying on its back on the porch, the sadder the house looked.

After a while, a thin gray cat crept up the steps and sat down by the door, its ears perked hopefully. When the door stayed shut, the cat hunkered down and tucked its paws under its chest. Closing its eyes, it dozed at its post.

Elizabeth smoothed Gordy's envelope. "Do you dare me to put this in the mail slot?"

I nodded, knowing she wanted me to encourage her.

Elizabeth looked up the street and down. No one was in sight. She leapt to her feet and ran up the sidewalk. Thrusting the letter through the mail slot, she thumped on the door and dashed back again. "Come on!"

I was already running as fast as I could. Heart thumping, feet pounding, gasping for breath, we raced around the corner and headed for home.

"Did anyone see us?" Elizabeth asked me after we'd gone into my room and slammed the door.

"Just the cat," I said. "You sure scared him. I never saw a cat disappear so fast."

We laughed then, just thinking about Gordy's cat, but later, after Elizabeth's mother called her home for dinner, it didn't seem so funny. Not just the cat, but the whole thing. Monday we would have to go to school and see Gordy. Even though we had the goods on him, as Elizabeth said, I was scared of what he might do.

*

A week passed without anything happening. Sometimes I thought Gordy was watching Elizabeth and me, but he didn't say a word to either of us. Or anybody else, for that matter. In fact, he spent most of the day with his head on his desk. He didn't cut up in class or cause trouble on the playground. Mrs. Wagner didn't keep him after school. Once she asked him if he was sick, but he just shook his head and stared at the floor. If I'd liked him, I would've been worried about him.

The next Saturday, Elizabeth and I were sitting in our tree, talking.

"I think our note scared Gordy pretty bad," Elizabeth said. "He hasn't said boo to anybody all week."

For a few minutes, she sat quietly, swinging one foot and frowning. The sun shone through her hair, changing it into a cloud of silver. I watched her warily, wondering what she was thinking about.

"Let's go down to the hut again and see what's going on," she said.

"Do we have to?" I asked, but she was already on the

ground, running toward the train tracks. Reluctantly, I swung down from the safety of our tree and ran after her.

Following our usual procedure, we crept close enough to see the hut. Except for a tiny trace of smoke from the chimney, the place looked deserted. No voices, no movement, no sound came from behind the closed door.

"I'll sneak up and look in the window," Elizabeth whispered. "You stay here and watch for Gordy."

"Be careful," I told Elizabeth, but she was already crawling toward the hut.

Nervously, I watched her cross the clearing on her hands and knees. When she was below the window, she rose slowly to her feet, and, while I held my breath, she peered inside. For a few seconds, nothing happened. Elizabeth didn't move, I didn't move, the squirrel who had hopped into the clearing behind Elizabeth didn't move. We were all as motionless as statues.

Then the woods behind me exploded with noise. Before I could shout a warning, Doug grabbed me, and Gordy was going after Elizabeth. She fought like a cat, furious, all fingernails and teeth, but she couldn't get away from him.

As we struggled, the hut's door opened, and Stuart ran outside. "Hey," he shouted. "What's going on? Let those girls go before you hurt them."

But Gordy and Doug ignored him. Shoving past Stuart, they dragged Elizabeth and me into the hut. Stuart followed us, and Gordy kicked the door shut. Blocking it with his body, he let go of Elizabeth.

"You sent that letter, didn't you?" Gordy yelled. His face was white, and the scar over his eyebrow was purple.

Quicker to recover than I was, Elizabeth glared at him. "So what if I did?" she panted, still breathing hard.

"Who else have you told?"

"That's for me to know and you to find out." She folded her arms across her chest and tipped her chin up.

"Didn't I tell you not to come down here?" Gordy yelled. "Didn't I warn you to stay out of the woods?"

"You aren't the boss of me," Elizabeth said, "and you don't own these woods."

"Hold on, Gordy." Stuart pulled his brother away from Elizabeth. "Leave her be. She's only a girl."

Nothing made Elizabeth madder than being called a girl. She clenched her fists and glared at Stuart, but he just laughed at her. "Aren't you Joe Crawford's little sister?" he asked.

"Don't you dare even speak my brother's name, you dirty deserter," Elizabeth said. "Joe's fighting the Japs right now. He's not hiding out in the woods, letting other people die for our country!"

Stuart stopped smiling then, and Elizabeth pointed at me. "Margaret's brother is in the war, too."

"I know," Stuart said. "So's my brother Donald."

"So how come you're not?" Elizabeth yelled.

Gordy grabbed Elizabeth and whirled her around so she was facing him. "You better not tell anybody about Stuart," he said.

"Why shouldn't I?" Elizabeth asked. "It's against the law to hide a deserter."

Gordy ran a hand through his hair, pushing it back from his forehead so it stood up like grass for a minute. Darting a look at Doug, he shoved his hands in his pockets and scowled at Elizabeth.

"Do you know what happens to deserters?" Gordy asked her. For once he didn't yell. Instead he leaned toward Elizabeth, almost like he was begging. "Stuart could be shot or put in jail or sent straight to the front. Some Nazi would kill him the first day. Do you want that to happen to him?"

"Huh," Elizabeth said. "It would serve him right." She flicked her eyes at Stuart. "I don't feel sorry for him, not one bit. I'd rather see him die than Joe."

She turned to me. "How about you, Margaret? Wouldn't you be mad if Jimmy died and old sissy baby Stuart was right here, safe in the woods?"

Without wanting to, I looked at Stuart. His long, dark hair hid most of his face, but I could see how thin he was. Like me, he was all elbows and knees and wrist bones. How could I wish him dead? I didn't want anybody to die. Not Jimmy, not Joe, not Stuart. I just wanted the war to be over.

When I didn't say anything, Stuart said, "There's been too much killing already. Even if they catch me and send me overseas, I won't shoot anybody. War's wrong."

"Tell Hitler about it," Elizabeth said scornfully. "He started it, not us. Him and the Japs. If we don't kill them, they'll kill us. Is that what you want?"

"Of course not," Stuart said. His voice faltered and he coughed. Running his hands through his hair, he looked at all of us. His face was very pale. "It's so complicated, I can't explain it. Killing's wrong. Wrong of them, wrong of us. I know it is."

Stuart stared at Elizabeth and me as if he hoped we'd understand what he meant, but we didn't say anything.

As Elizabeth said, America hadn't started the war. Like it or not, we had to stop Hitler. Everybody knew that.

"Look," Stuart tried again. "The Germans and the Japs and the Italians are all people, right? Just like us. They have mothers and fathers, they have wives, they have little kids. They don't want to kill me any more than I want to kill them. They just want to live their lives and let me live mine. You know, tell a few jokes, sit in the sun, eat dinner, go for a walk, stuff like that. Same as us."

Elizabeth turned to me. "You were right after all, Margaret. There really is a crazy man in the woods."

Stuart shoved his hands deep in his pockets and lowered his head. He looked so confused and unhappy I couldn't help feeling sorry for him.

I glanced at Gordy to see if he understood what Stuart was trying to say, but he was leaning against the door, scowling at the ground and shaking his head. He didn't agree with Stuart any more than Elizabeth did.

"You're just a sissy." Elizabeth scowled at Stuart. "Like my brother always said you were. Isn't he, Margaret?"

Since Elizabeth expected me to agree with her, I nodded, but I felt as if a crack had opened in the solid earth under my feet. When Jimmy was drafted, I'd never thought to ask him how he felt about going to war. Until now, it hadn't occurred to me that he might not want to kill anyone. In fact, I'd never really thought about his pointing a gun at a human being and pulling the trigger. How could Jimmy do that? How could anyone?

Silence filled the hut, sucking in the air, suffocating us. Nobody spoke, nobody moved. Outside the wind rattled the treetops and sneaked through the cracks between the boards. Its cold currents circled our ankles and crept down our necks. Like a noise offstage, a train blew its whistle for the Calvert Road crossing. Once, twice, three times, getting louder each time. When the engine thundered past, it drowned out the sound of the wind and shook the hut's walls.

I studied Stuart's pale face and tried to understand. Was war something you could walk away from like a fight on the playground? Shivering in the cold, I wished Jimmy was here so I could ask him what he thought. If anyone could explain, he could. My brother knew everything.

12

In the quiet the train left behind, Gordy looked at Elizabeth and me. "Promise you won't tell," he said. "Stuart can't fight, he never could. He'd be a lousy soldier."

Stuart glanced at his brother. "How many times do I have to tell you? Fighting's not everything, Gordy."

Ignoring Stuart, Gordy kept his eyes on Elizabeth and me, waiting for us to speak.

Elizabeth tilted her head and peered at Gordy through a tangle of hair. "What's it worth to you for us to keep our mouths shut?"

Gordy and Doug exchanged looks. "We'll leave you alone," Gordy said. "We'll quit picking on you."

"How about those boards you stole from us?" Elizabeth asked. "How about our tree house?"

"We'll build you another one," Gordy muttered. "Better than that crummy thing you had."

"What do you think, Margaret?" Elizabeth asked.

"Sounds okay to me," I said. All I really wanted to do was get out of that hut and go home. I'd have agreed to anything just to escape. I didn't want to hear another word from Stuart, I didn't want to look at his sad face. Most of all, I didn't want to feel sorry for him.

"All right," Elizabeth said to Gordy. "But you better build us the best tree house in College Hill."

"Promise not to say nothing about Stuart." Gordy glared at us, but he was beaten. He knew it, and we knew it.

"Cross my heart and hope to die, if I ever tell a lie," we said.

"Now get out of here," Gordy said, a little bit of the old menace creeping into his voice. "And don't come back."

He stepped aside and opened the door. Elizabeth walked out first, but I hesitated. Stuart was coughing. It sounded deep and loose, like it was coming from way down in his chest.

"Is he all right?" I asked Gordy.

"Scram, Magpie," Gordy said. "I can take care of Stuart. I don't need any stupid girls hanging around!"

He looked out the door at Elizabeth. "You, too, Lizard!" he shouted. "Get lost, both of you!"

Without looking back, Elizabeth and I raced for home. When we were safely across the train tracks, Elizabeth turned to me.

"Aren't you glad we went down there?" she asked. "Now we have Gordy right where we want him."

I twisted a braid around one finger and looked up at the sky. It was blue and clear. You could see straight up, through miles and miles of air, maybe all the way to heaven if your eyes were only sharp enough to recognize it.

"Do you think our brothers wanted to go to war?" I asked Elizabeth.

"Of course," she said. "They're not cowards like Stuart."

"But what he said about killing. Do you think he's right?"

"Don't be stupid, Margaret. The Nazis and the Japs want to take over the whole world. Look at all the people they've killed. Not just soldiers like Butch and Harold, but old men, women, children, little babies. We have to stop them. If everybody acted like Stuart, Hitler would be in the White House right now. Is that what you want?"

"No. I hate Hitler just as much as you do."

Elizabeth stared at me. "Well, then, forget what Stuart said. He's a sissy, that's all. Sometimes you have to fight, you can't just let bad things happen."

I shivered as a cold edge of wind worked its way down my neck. With all my heart, I wished Hitler was dead and the war was over and my brother was safe at home. Then nobody would have to kill anybody else, nobody would have to die.

*

On Sunday afternoon, I was out in the backyard helping Mother hang out the laundry when Elizabeth showed up at my back gate with Gordy, Doug, and Toad. Gordy's wagon was piled high with boards, and Toad was carrying a coffee can full of nails. Where they found so much stuff was anybody's guess. I hoped they hadn't stolen it.

Taking the clothespins out of her mouth, Mother smiled at Gordy. "Well, well," she said. "I haven't seen you since you used to tag along behind Stuart and Donald. If I'm not mistaken, they pulled you all over College Hill in that wagon when you were knee-high to a grasshopper."

Doug and Toad laughed, and Gordy actually blushed. Unaware of his embarrassment, Mother went right on talking.

"Seems like yesterday all the boys were playing here in the backyard," she said. "Jimmy, Joe, Donald, Stuart,

Butch, Harold. And you, watching them from the wagon. Lord, how time flies."

Mother focused on Gordy again, noticed his red face, and finally realized he wasn't the kind of boy who liked to be reminded he was once a little kid riding in a wagon.

"How are your brothers?" she asked to change the subject. "Do you hear from them regularly?"

Gordy nodded. "They're fine."

"Well, you be sure and tell Stuart how much I miss him. He was the best paperboy we ever had. No matter what the weather was like, he never missed a day."

"Yes, ma'am," Gordy said, but it was me he was looking at. Worried I might let the cat out of the bag, I suppose.

"Gordy's here to help Elizabeth and me build a new tree house," I told Mother. "Do you need me anymore?"

"No, we've gotten all the sheets up. All that's left is underwear. I can manage that by myself. You run along, Margaret."

And I did, as fast as I could, praying Gordy hadn't noticed the pink panties Mother was pegging to the line.

*

Despite ourselves, Elizabeth and I were impressed at how quickly the boys nailed the platform together. Much as we hated to admit it, the new tree house was bigger and better than the old one. When it was finished, all five of us had room to sit, legs dangling, eating the apples Mother brought out to us.

"So how long is Stuart going to hide over there?" Elizabeth gestured with her apple at the woods.

"Till the war's over," Gordy mumbled.

"That could be a long, long time," Elizabeth said.

We all nodded and swung our legs. Toad challenged Doug and Gordy to an apple seed–spitting contest. Uninvited, Elizabeth joined in and won. It was very warm for December. The boys' jackets hung over tree limbs, and Elizabeth's pea coat was unbuttoned. Her curls fluffed around her face as she turned to Gordy with more questions.

"Do you agree with Stuart?" she asked. "About killing being wrong, no matter what?"

"Hell, no," Gordy said, daring anybody to tell him not to cuss. "The only good Nazi's a dead Nazi. And that's true of the Japs, too. Stuart's got some crackpot ideas."

"Then how come you're hiding him?" Elizabeth wanted to know. "Why don't you turn him in?"

"He might be nuts," Gordy said, "but he's my brother."

Elizabeth swung her head toward Doug and Toad. "What about you-all? Stuart's not your brother. Don't you think it's wrong to hide a deserter?"

Toad shot a look at Gordy and shrugged. There was no way he'd go against his leader. "Stu's a good guy," he said. "A little dumb, maybe, but nice. If he doesn't want to go to war, it's okay with me."

When Elizabeth turned to him, Doug frowned and shoved his hair out of his face. "It might be against the law," he said, "but I've known Stu a long time. I got no reason to turn him in."

Doug paused and glared at Elizabeth through narrowed eyes. "You got no reason either," he said. "Stu never did anything to hurt you, did he?"

"Hurt's got nothing to do with it," Elizabeth said. "If

you ask me, Stuart's scared of being killed so he made up some highfalutin reason for not going to war. Did you ever think of that?" As she spoke, Elizabeth wisely put some distance between herself and Gordy.

"Stuart's no coward." Gordy leaned toward Elizabeth, his face red with anger. "He's taken more than one beating for me."

Elizabeth stared at him. "Does your father beat you?" she asked. "Is that how you got that black eye?"

"Shut up, Lizard. I'm sick of your stupid questions. Just mind your own beeswax and let me worry about my brother, okay?"

Grabbing a limb, Gordy swung out of the tree, and Toad and Doug followed him. Pulling the empty wagon behind them, they sauntered up the alley toward Dartmoor Avenue.

"Dumbo!" Elizabeth shouted at them.

The only response she got was a dirty gesture from Gordy.

Turning to me, she said, "I hate Gordy. If his father beats him, he probably deserves it. Maybe we should turn Stuart in after all."

"Oh, no, Elizabeth," I said. "We promised not to. And besides," I added, "Gordy would kill us if we did, and you know it."

Elizabeth frowned and buttoned her pea coat. The sun was resting on the treetops, getting ready to dive down into the dark, and I shivered as I zipped my jacket.

"You're right," she said reluctantly. Then she grinned. "Well, at least we got a good tree house out of them."

13

In the middle of the week, the weather turned much colder. On the way to school, the wind slashed me to the bone and made my ears ache. For once, I was happy to race inside the building and take my seat near the radiator. The waves of heat made my legs itch under my high wool socks, but I was glad for the warmth.

While Mrs. Wagner went over our arithmetic problems, I thought about Stuart in his hut in the woods. The little stove Gordy had rigged up didn't look like it would put out enough heat to make up for the cold air whistling through the cracks. I imagined Stuart huddled under blankets, shivering and coughing. Suppose he got really sick?

I looked around the room for Gordy. That was when I noticed he was absent. He'd been out yesterday, too, I realized. As much as he hated school, Gordy was usually present. He must be pretty sick to miss a couple of days, I thought.

While I gazed out the window, thinking about Stuart and Gordy, I gradually became aware of a silence all around me. No pages rustled, no desks squeaked, no voices spoke. Uncomfortably, I forced myself to look at Mrs. Wagner. Just as I feared, she was staring at me, a frown creasing her forehead.

"Do you know the answer, Margaret?" she asked.

"No, ma'am," I whispered. I didn't even know the question, let alone the answer.

All around me, people whispered the page number and the question, but I was too upset to understand anything they said. I just sat there, my head lowered, feeling stupid.

Other kids raised their hands and waved them at Mrs. Wagner, eager to show her they'd been paying attention. Unlike me, they knew both the question and the answer.

"Page sixty-three, Margaret," Mrs. Wagner said patiently. "Question five."

With fumbly fingers, I turned to the right page and started at question five. "Jimmy has seven apples," I read. "He wants to share them equally with his three friends. What is the best way to do this?"

I shook my head. The problem seemed insurmountable. I had no idea what Jimmy should do. Maybe some of his friends weren't hungry. Maybe one or two of them didn't even like apples. The only Jimmy I knew was somewhere in France or Belgium. I was pretty sure he wasn't worrying about apples.

"Please pay attention," Mrs. Wagner said. "I'll call on you later, Margaret."

Leaving me to worry about the question she'd ask me next, I listened to Doug give the correct answer.

After school, I asked Elizabeth if she'd noticed Gordy had been absent for two days in a row. "I hope he doesn't have anything contagious," I said. "Last Sunday we were sitting right next to him."

Elizabeth frowned for a moment. We were walking along the trolley tracks, and, as usual, she was trying to balance on a rail. Even with her arms outspread, the wind was making her wobble. Giving up, she put one foot on the gravel and turned to me.

"Maybe Stuart's gotten worse," she said, "and Gordy's taking care of him."

I stared at Elizabeth, bracing myself for what she might say next. The wind tugged at my braids, and I shivered.

"Let's go to Gordy's house," she said, "and see if he's sick. We can tell his mother Mrs. Wagner asked us to give him his homework. I've always wanted to see what his house is like inside."

Without giving me a chance to say a word, Elizabeth ran up the trolley tracks toward Davis Road, and I dashed after her. When we reached Gordy's house, Elizabeth paused, took a deep breath, and marched up the sidewalk. The same naked baby doll lay on the porch, and the same cat waited by the door. When it saw us, it meowed hopefully and watched Elizabeth press the bell.

For a few minutes, nothing happened. The cat rubbed against my legs and purred, and the wind rattled the bare tree limbs. From the yard next door, a dog barked at us.

"Maybe the bell doesn't work," I said. What I was hoping was that no one was home. The longer we stood on Gordy's porch, the more scared I grew. Suppose Mr. Smith came to the door and yelled at us?

Elizabeth knocked hard, and I began edging away. As I teetered on the top step, I heard someone moving around inside the house. I wanted to run, but I knew Elizabeth would never forgive me if I did.

While I stood there, a thin woman opened the door and stared at us. She was holding a baby on one hip, an older girl clung to her skirt, and behind her were two little boys, miniatures of Gordy. Something about Mrs. Smith scared me, and I took a step or two away from her, treading on the cat's paw as I did so. When it meowed, I bent down to pet it, glad for an excuse to lower my eyes.

"Is Gordy here?" Elizabeth asked.

"He's not home from school yet," Mrs. Smith said. Her voice was flat and unfriendly. She neither frowned nor smiled. Even the baby looked sullen and suspicious.

Elizabeth and I glanced at each other. Without knowing it, Mrs. Smith had just told us where Gordy probably was.

"You have a nice cat," I said, hoping to make her smile.

"That scrawny old thing?" Mrs. Smith frowned at the cat, but the little girl opened the screen door.

"Mittens, come here," she called as it ran inside, dodging the fingers reaching out to grab it.

"Shut the door, stupid," a man's voice rumbled from inside. "You trying to freeze me to death?"

As Mrs. Smith glanced behind her, Elizabeth stared through the screen door. I knew she was dying to go inside and see everything in Gordy's house, including the owner of the deep, nasty voice.

Just as Mrs. Smith started to close the door, a man strode down the hall toward us. He was tall and skinny, as pale as Gordy and Stuart, and his eyes were small and mean. In one hand, he held the squirming cat by the nape of its neck. The little girl ran behind him, crying.

Mrs. Smith stepped aside as he opened the screen door and hurled the cat past Elizabeth and me. Horrified, I watched it fly through the air, land on all four feet, and run off through a hole in the hedge.

"I told you not to let that thing in the house!" the man yelled.

Mrs. Smith cringed, the little kids began to cry, and the girl ran down the steps barefoot and coatless, calling for the cat.

"Come back here, June!" Mr. Smith shouted.

The girl stopped halfway down the sidewalk. Her nose was running, and tears streaked her cheeks. "I hate you!" she cried. "I hate you!"

Mr. Smith looked at Elizabeth and me as if he'd just noticed us. "What the hell do you want?" he asked. "If you're selling magazines, we don't want any."

"They were looking for Gordy," Mrs. Smith said timidly.

"Well, he's not here." Pulling his wife inside, Mr. Smith slammed the door, leaving Elizabeth and me on the porch and June on the sidewalk.

Elizabeth and I stared at June, and she stared back. With a dirty fist, she wiped her tears away, but she didn't move. She stood on the sidewalk and scowled at us as if we were responsible for the entire episode.

Glancing behind me at the closed door, I walked down the steps and knelt on the sidewalk in front of June. Looking into her gray eyes, I said, "The cat's all right. He landed on his feet and ran through the hedge."

"She's a girl," June said scornfully. "Her name is Mittens." Even though she was just a little kid, June sounded exactly like Gordy.

"Want us to find her for you?" Elizabeth asked.

Before June had a chance to answer, Gordy rode into the yard on his bike. Skidding to a stop, he stared at Elizabeth and me. For the first time since I'd known him, he looked scared.

"What are you doing here?" he asked. "Did you tell?"

Elizabeth scowled at Gordy. "Of course not," she said. "We just wondered where you were."

Gordy looked at June. "Where's your coat? You don't even have shoes on!"

June threw her arms around Gordy and started crying. "Daddy was mean to Mittens again. He threw her off the porch. Then he slammed the door. If I go in there, he'll whip me."

Gordy picked up June and looked at us over the top of her head. "Get out of here," he said, "before I bust your lip!"

"Don't make me go in there," June sobbed. "I don't want to see Daddy no more."

But Gordy was carrying her up the front steps, stroking her hair and telling her not to cry. "I'll take care of you," he said. Then he turned to Elizabeth and me. "Didn't you hear me?" he yelled. "Get out of my yard, you dopes!"

This time Elizabeth and I listened. Without another word, we turned and ran.

14

As soon as we were far enough away from Gordy's house to feel safe, Elizabeth and I slowed down to a walk. For a few minutes we trudged along silently, trying to breathe normally. Never had a grown man scared me as much as Mr. Smith had . . . not even the crazy man. Now that it was too late, I wished I'd never gone near Davis Road. There were some things you were better off not knowing about, I thought, and Mr. Smith was one of them.

Elizabeth was the first to speak. "I wish Daddy could throw Mr. Smith in jail forever," she said. "That's where he belongs."

"Do you think he always acts like that?" I asked.

"He must've been d-r-u-n-k." Imitating her mother, Elizabeth spelled it out. "That's what's wrong with him."

Tipping her head back, Elizabeth pretended to drink from a bottle. Then she staggered across the sidewalk, fell against a telephone pole, and made a loud hiccuping sound. I knew she wanted me to laugh, but somehow it wasn't funny, not now, not after seeing Mr. Smith throw the cat and yell at everybody.

Changing the subject, I reminded Elizabeth that we'd gone to the Smiths' house to find out why Gordy hadn't been in school. "I bet you were right," I said. "Stuart must be worse and Gordy played hooky to take care of him."

"Let's find out," Elizabeth said.

Although I would have preferred to go home, I followed her across the train tracks and into the woods. The scraggly arms of thornbushes lashed my face and caught at my clothes and hair, and the wind blustered through the treetops, pushing us toward the hut. By the time Elizabeth and I reached the clearing, we were both out of breath.

The door was shut, and no one was in sight. In the wintry dusk, the hut looked like something from a fairy tale, a place where a witch might live. I hung back a moment, but Elizabeth shoved the door open and went inside.

From the threshold, I saw the glow of the railroad lantern. A fire burned in the little stove, warming the air slightly but not enough to dispel the odor of kerosene, damp earth, and old wool.

Draped in blankets, Stuart sat on the cot and stared at us. He was coughing, and, even in the dim light, I saw the dark shadows under his eyes. His cheeks were hollowed out, and he shivered.

"Are you okay?" Elizabeth asked.

Stuart shook his head and coughed again. "Is Gordy with you?" His voice was so hoarse I could barely hear him.

"No," Elizabeth said, "it's just me and Margaret." Walking closer, she stared hard at Stuart. "You look awful."

"Thanks," Stuart whispered.

"You need a doctor," Elizabeth went on, "and medicine."

"I don't think doctors make house calls to bums in the woods." Stuart tried to laugh, but he started coughing and ruined the humor of it.

"I'll bring you some Cheracol," I said. "We've got some left from the last time I was sick."

Stuart shook his head. He was probably afraid to say anything for fear of making himself cough again.

"How about aspirin?" I asked, trying to remember what Mother gave me when I felt bad. "Ginger ale and soup," I added. "You need them, too."

Elizabeth and I looked around the hut. There wasn't much food. A few cans of pork and beans, a jug of water, a jar of applesauce, half a loaf of bread, some peanut butter.

"Does Gordy bring you dinner?" Elizabeth asked.

"Sometimes," Stuart said. "When he can."

Elizabeth looked at me and sighed. "Well," she said to Stuart, "I guess we'll just have to make sure you get more stuff. I don't think Gordy's doing a very good job."

That made Stuart smile. "Who do you think you are?" he asked. "Florence Nightingale?"

Elizabeth scowled. "Just because I'm a girl, you think I can't do anything."

"I never said that," Stuart said. "In fact, you're a pretty unusual girl."

"I am, aren't I?" Elizabeth smiled. "I never cry and nothing scares me," she said with her usual modesty.

"Not even Gordy?"

"He's a dumbo," Elizabeth said scornfully.

"How about you?" Stuart turned to me. "Are you brave too, Margaret?"

Looking at my feet, I let Elizabeth answer for me.

"She's a sissy baby sometimes," Elizabeth admitted, "but mostly she's okay. Once I talk her into something, she does it. Like coming here. By herself, she never would

97

have done it, but with me, well, she's braver. Right, Margaret?"

She smiled at me then, and I nodded so hard my braids thunked my shoulders. It was true. With Elizabeth beside me, I wasn't nearly so scared of things.

Stuart looked at Elizabeth. "So how come you want to help me all of a sudden?" he asked. "The last time you saw me you said you hoped I'd die. Remember?"

Elizabeth blushed. "Well, I still think if my brother has to go to war, you should go too, but I don't want you to die. Not really. I just said that because I was mad." She shoved her fists into the pockets of her pea coat and frowned.

Stuart smiled, but even under his blankets, he was trembling with cold. For a few seconds, there was no sound but the wind.

"Do you know my old man?" Stuart asked suddenly.

"We just met him today," Elizabeth said. "For the very first time."

And the last, I hoped, but I didn't say that out loud.

"Do you know what he'd do if he found out Gordy was helping me?" Stuart went on.

Elizabeth shook her head, and Stuart said, "He'd beat him black and blue. He told Gordy he'd like to see me dead or spending the rest of my life busting rock in an army prison camp. As far as he's concerned, I should be shot at dawn."

"Your father knows you deserted?" Elizabeth asked.

Stuart nodded. "The army told him. When I didn't come back from furlough last summer, they came to the house looking for me, but Gordy hid me down here. Nobody else knows where I am. They think I'm hundreds of miles away by now."

He shivered again as a blast of wind swept through the cracks in the wall behind him. Even with a beard hiding half his face, he reminded me of his mother. He had the same sad, worn-down look about him. Only he didn't scare me like she did.

"Gordy wants to take care of me all by himself," Stuart said, "but the old man's bound to get suspicious if he keeps on stealing food and playing hooky. I made him promise to go to school tomorrow. When you see him, tell him it's okay for you to help me, I want you to."

Stuart started coughing again. "You better get going," he said. "It's almost dark. You never know who might be hiding in the woods, do you?"

He grinned to show us he was joking, but when Elizabeth and I left the hut, the woods were full of shadows, and the wind was making scary sounds in the treetops.

Without saying a word, we ran all the way home. Pausing at my gate, Elizabeth scuffed at the cinders Daddy dumped in the alley whenever he cleaned the furnace. "We aren't ever going to tell anyone about Stuart," Elizabeth said fiercely. "No matter what."

Behind her, the sunset had turned the clouds fiery red and purple, and it looked as if the whole world were going up in flames. The white sides of houses and garages were pink, and the puddles in the alley were sheets of crimson. Even the glass in the windows was scarlet, as if fires raged inside.

I stared at her, momentarily surprised by her sudden change of attitude. I should have expected it. That was how Elizabeth was. Her opinions veered back and forth like a weather vane on a rooftop. What she hated one day, she loved the next.

"The way I see it, Stuart is our secret," Elizabeth went on. "Yours and mine. Nobody else knows except Gordy and Doug and Toad."

She paused, her eyes wide, and dropped her voice to a whisper. "Stuart's life is in our hands, Margaret." To demonstrate, Elizabeth extended her red mittens, palms up. "His very life."

Then she was gone, leaping the puddles and running up her back steps.

"Where have you been?" Mother asked as I opened the kitchen door. "It's almost dark."

"In the alley, talking to Elizabeth."

"Your father will be home any minute," she said. Thrusting a handful of knives, forks, and spoons at me, she told me to set the table. Then, without another word, she turned her attention to the potatoes bubbling on the stove.

The set of her back told me this wasn't the time to ask her any of the questions filling my head. We hadn't gotten a letter from Jimmy for days, and she was tense with worry.

*

After dinner, while Daddy was listening to H. V. Kaltenborn's commentary on the war, I sat down across from Mother at the kitchen table. She looked up from the socks she was darning. "Have you finished your homework?" she asked.

"Yes," I said, "but I wanted to talk to you about something."

"Well?"

I ran my finger along the edge of the table. "Did you know Mr. Smith beats Gordy?"

Mother worked her needle through the heel of Daddy's sock, closing the hole he'd worn in it. "Mr. Smith is Gordy's father," she said. "He knows what's best for his son. Maybe that's the only way he can make Gordy behave."

"But he gave him a black eye," I said.

Mother looked up from the sock. "Do you know that for a fact, Margaret?"

I rubbed my finger back and forth, back and forth, making a squeaking sound on the table's enameled surface. Somehow I thought Mother would be outraged at the very thought of a father beating his son. Daddy never hit Jimmy or me. Or even yelled at us. Once in a while Mother gave me a whack on the bottom with a hairbrush, but it didn't really hurt.

"June says her father hits them," I said. "And he threw their cat out the door. I saw him do it."

"What people do in their homes is their own business. It's not for us to interfere." Picking up another sock, Mother frowned at me. "What were you doing at the Smiths' house, anyway? That's not the sort of place I want you spending your time."

"We were just walking by," I said.

"You saw all this just walking by their house?"

I nodded, and Mother leaned toward me. "Stay away from the Smiths," she said. "You and Elizabeth both. I'm sure Mrs. Crawford feels the same way I do."

"You were nice to Gordy on Sunday," I said. "You told him Stuart was the best paperboy you ever had."

"I don't mind Gordy coming here," Mother said. "I just don't want you going there. I never let Jimmy play at their house, and you can't either."

Glancing at the kitchen clock, Mother stopped me from asking any more questions by telling me it was past my bedtime.

Disappointed, I trudged up the steps to my room. It seemed to me Mother should be more concerned. Something was wrong at the Smiths' house, but all she cared about was not being a busybody.

Snuggling under my covers, I listened to the wind knock against my window. Here I was warm and safe, but Stuart was sick and alone in his hut in the woods, and Mr. Smith was scaring June and his wife and all those little kids. Maybe at this very moment he was beating Gordy. How did it feel to be socked so hard your eye turned black? Did it hurt enough to make even a boy as tough as Gordy cry?

15

*A*t three-thirty the next day, Elizabeth and I waited outside school for Gordy. Suspecting he'd been playing hooky, Mrs. Wagner had kept him in to catch up on his lessons. When he shoved the big green door open and saw Elizabeth and me, he frowned.

"What are you jerks hanging around here for?" he said. "You want a punch in the face or something?"

He walked down the steps, his fists clenched. He looked so menacing, I wanted to run, but Elizabeth grabbed my sleeve and stopped me from going anywhere.

"Didn't I warn you, Lizard?" Gordy shoved his face close to Elizabeth's. "Quit spying. You're going to ruin everything!"

Elizabeth's head tilted back, but she didn't budge. "Stuart wants us to help," she said. "He asked me to tell you."

"Liar. He never said nothing like that." Gordy glared at her. "You want the army to get him. I bet you already told everybody in College Hill where he is."

"Don't you dare call me a tattletale!" Elizabeth stood on her tiptoes, making herself eye to eye with Gordy. "I feel sorry for Stuart. He's sick. He needs people to watch over him and bring him things. You can't do it all by yourself."

Gordy sniffed and ran the back of his hand past his

nose. The wind whipped his hair, and he looked cold and miserable. The scar above his eyebrow made a livid streak against his pale skin. For the first time I wondered how he'd gotten it.

"We can take food to him," Elizabeth went on. "And maybe even medicine. Suppose he dies? What would you do? Bury him in the woods all by your stupid self?"

"You shut up!" Gordy drew back one arm, and I thought for sure he was going to punch Elizabeth. She didn't even duck. She just stood there glaring at him, daring him to hit her.

Turning aside, Gordy shoved both fists into his jacket pockets. He stood there for a few moments, his head down, his shoulders slumped. When he looked up, I thought I saw the glitter of tears in his eyes, but it was probably my imagination.

"Okay," he muttered. "If Stuart really wants you to help, get some food and meet me at the hut." Yanking his bike out of the rack, he vaulted on like a cowboy and pedaled away. We watched him till he turned the corner by the trolley tracks, but he didn't look back.

"Come on." Elizabeth ran across the playground with me in pursuit. When we got to our block, she slowed down and pulled me close so she could whisper in my ear.

"You get aspirin and cough syrup," she told me. "I'll bring food. Chicken soup with rice if we have it. Then meet me in the alley. Be sure no one sees you."

I nodded and raced for home. Mother was in the kitchen listening to "Stella Dallas" while she fixed dinner. She was so absorbed in Stella's latest sorrow she barely noticed me run up to my room.

Changing my clothes as fast as I could, I slipped into the bathroom and grabbed a little bottle of aspirin and the cough medicine. Dropping them into my jacket pocket, I hurried down the hall and sauntered into the kitchen, trying to look like my ordinary everyday self, not a girl hiding stolen goods.

"How about some Ovaltine to warm you up?" Mother asked.

"Elizabeth is waiting for me," I said. Through the window in the back door, I could see her stamping the ice on a mud puddle. She liked the tinkling sound it made when it broke.

Without giving Mother a chance to ask any more questions, I hurried out into the cold air and joined Elizabeth.

"Did you get the medicine?" she asked me as we ran down the alley.

When I nodded, Elizabeth said, "Good. I got some soup and a can of stew and a jar of applesauce. Nice nourishing food. Maybe we can fatten Stuart up."

By the time Elizabeth and I got to the hut, Gordy and Doug had lit a small campfire in the clearing. With stony faces, they watched us approach.

Reaching into my pockets, I held the aspirin and cough medicine out like offerings. Without even saying thanks, Gordy grabbed the soup from Elizabeth and looked at the labels. While we watched, he opened a can, dumped the soup into a small pot, and plunked it down in the fire.

Leaving him there, Elizabeth and I went into the hut. Stuart was lying on the cot, covered with blankets. His face was flushed, and his eyes were glittery. When he saw Elizabeth and me, he smiled and tried to sit up. The effort made him cough.

"You look sicker," Elizabeth said, tactful as ever. She took the Cheracol from me and poured some into a spoon. Like a little kid, Stuart opened his mouth wide, and Elizabeth tipped the medicine down his throat.

"Ugh," he said.

"The worse it tastes, the better it is for you," Elizabeth told him. "At least, that's what my mother always says."

Next she made him take two aspirins and drink a glass of water. "You'll be better soon," she told him.

Stuart nodded. "You make it sound like a threat," he said, but he smiled to show her he was kidding.

Then the door thumped open, and Gordy came in carrying the pot of soup. "It's real hot," he told Stuart as he carefully set it on the orange-crate table.

Stuart stirred the soup and blew on a spoonful. When he swallowed, he winced as if it hurt his throat. After he'd eaten about half the soup, he lay down and pulled the covers up to his chin.

"See?" he said to Gordy. "I told you the girls would be a big help."

Gordy didn't say anything. Without looking at Elizabeth or me, he bent over Stuart. "Should we go now?" he asked his brother.

Stuart nodded. "You don't want the old man looking for you," he said. "Don't make him mad, Gordy. I'm not worth it."

Silently, we followed Gordy outside. Doug had dumped water on the fire, and the smell of damp ashes lingered in the clearing. He and Gordy walked ahead of us through the trees. Side by side, heads down, hands jammed in their pockets, saying nothing, they looked like old men.

"We'll come again tomorrow," Elizabeth said before the boys turned off in the direction of their homes.

Gordy looked at us then. "Stuart's getting sicker and sicker," he said, his voice rising until he was yelling at us. "Somebody should be with him all day, making sure he's okay. I can't keep missing school. Mrs. Wagner called my mother and she told my father. Do you know what he'll do to me if I play hooky again?"

Elizabeth and I stared at Gordy. The sun was a red ball behind him, and his shadow stretched toward us, ending in a pinhead at our feet.

"I'll do it," Elizabeth said. "I can forge a note for Mrs. Wagner. I'm real good at disguising my handwriting."

She watched Gordy, waiting for his approval. He chewed his lower lip and studied the ground. Finally, he looked up and sighed.

"Okay," he said. "But if anything goes wrong, it's your fault, Lizard. I'll personally make you very sorry."

Elizabeth took a deep breath. I couldn't tell if she was relieved or scared. Looking Gordy in the eye, she said, "Nothing will go wrong."

"It better not," Gordy said. Without another word, he and Doug trudged off into the sunset.

Elizabeth and I watched them until they turned the corner. A gust of wind whipped my braids, and I shivered. "You can't go down there all by yourself," I said.

"Why not?" Elizabeth tossed her hair out of her eyes.

"Suppose your parents find out?"

"They won't," she said.

"I'll come with you," I said, hardly daring to think about what I was saying.

Elizabeth seized my hands and jumped up and down. "Oh, Margaret, that's great! I didn't think you would. I was scared even to ask you!"

Wondering what I'd done, I watched Elizabeth run up her back steps. I'd never played hooky, and I was terrified of what might happen if we were caught, but I couldn't let Elizabeth do it all by herself. She was my friend, and I had to stick by her no matter what.

Quietly, I slipped into the house, hoping Mother wouldn't take one look at me and know exactly what I was planning to do. My face always gave everything away.

I needn't have worried. As usual, Mother was too busy to pay much attention to me. If I was quieter than normal at dinner, neither she nor Daddy noticed. They had more important things on their minds.

The Germans had started a big campaign against us in France and Belgium, and things looked worse every day. Mrs. Wagner told us about it in school. Pointing to a place on the map called the Ardennes, she said that was where we were fighting the Battle of the Bulge. According to Daddy, Jimmy was probably right in the middle of it, and he and Mother talked of nothing else.

16

*T*he next morning, Elizabeth and I walked up Garfield Road just as if it were an ordinary day and we were going to school. At the trolley tracks, though, we stopped and looked ahead. Way up the street, under a gray sky heavy with clouds, we saw Polly, Linda, and Judy. Ducking behind a telephone pole, we watched them pause to talk to Bruce and then run across the playground. As the cold wind swirled around me, I wished with all my heart that Elizabeth and I were with them.

A screech of tires startled us. Whirling around, we saw Gordy on his bike. "You didn't tell me Baby Magpie was going with you," he said to Elizabeth.

While I stood there wishing people would stop thinking I was a baby, Elizabeth leapt to my defense. Glaring at Gordy, she said, "Margaret's not going to blab on Stuart any more than I am."

The wind blew Gordy's hair in and out of his eyes, and he tossed his head to the side, considering Elizabeth and me.

"Just make sure nobody follows you," he said at last. "As soon as school's out, me and Toad and Doug will come down there and you can go home."

Gordy looked around as if he expected to see spies everywhere, just waiting to catch Stuart. "Go on," he said, "before I change my mind and sock you a good one."

He pedaled toward school, glancing back from time to time to scowl at us. Checking to make sure there were no tattletales in sight, Elizabeth and I ran down the trolley tracks, putting a couple of streets between us and Garfield before we cut up an alley toward the woods.

*

By the time we got to the hut, we were out of breath and freezing cold. Stuart was lying so still under a pile of ragged blankets, I was afraid we were too late, but when Elizabeth bent over him, he opened his eyes and smiled at her.

"Well, well," he said, "look who's here, the angel of the battlefield." His voice was low and husky, and his eyes were bright and sparkly. Despite his beard and long, shaggy hair, he looked very handsome, but I remembered Mother telling me once I looked too pretty to be well. Sticking a thermometer in my mouth, she'd put me to bed. Sure enough my rosy cheeks and bright eyes were the result of a high fever, and I'd spent the next couple of weeks in bed with strep throat.

Relying on what we'd learned in Girl Scouts, Elizabeth and I managed to get a fire going so we could make tea for Stuart. After he drank it, he looked better, but he was coughing a lot.

Elizabeth and I had used the money we'd been saving for Christmas presents to buy three boxes of cough drops and a big bottle of Cheracol. After pouring a couple of spoonfuls of cough syrup down his throat, Elizabeth gave

Stuart a handful of little yellow lozenges and sat down beside him.

"Tell me something." Elizabeth stared at Stuart. "Did you go all the way through boot camp and then change your mind about fighting?"

Stuart shut his eyes for a moment as if he were trying to remember something that had happened a long, long time ago. "I didn't want to serve in the army," he said, "and I was thinking about becoming a conscientious objector or something. But while I was making up my mind, I got drafted and then I thought maybe I should be in the army like everybody else. I never hated anything so much in my whole life."

I thought about the funny letters Jimmy sent us from boot camp. He'd made Fort Benning sound like a joke, but maybe if you were actually there doing all that stuff you wouldn't find it so comical. Especially if you weren't good at sports or fighting.

"Finally I came home on furlough," Stuart went on, "but I knew the next step would be a ship going to Europe. Then I got this letter from Donald. It was different from the ones he sent the old man. He told me his outfit shot down three or four English planes by mistake, and then fired on one of our own divisions. He said it happened all the time. They were always making mistakes, shelling towns, killing civilians, families."

Stuart coughed, long and hard. When he stopped, he reached under his cot and pulled out a metal box. In it was a letter written on familiar V-mail stationery, creased and recreased from being read over and over again. Stuart smoothed it out and read, " 'Don't believe that patriotic stuff about dying for your country. All me and my buddies want to do is get out of this mess alive. War is nothing but killing people before they kill you, and it's more awful than anything you can imagine.' "

"*Donald* wrote that?" Elizabeth stared at Stuart.

Stuart put the letter back in his box and coughed again, even harder this time. He lay back on his cot and closed his eyes. "There's no way I can believe war is the answer to anything," he said.

Elizabeth and I looked at each other. Nobody said a word. Jimmy never wrote about the war itself, though sometimes, like Mother said, he sounded unhappy and homesick. Was he keeping thoughts like Donald's to himself?

I wanted to ask Stuart if the war was like that for everybody in Europe, but he was asleep. He wasn't coughing, but his breath was loud and rattly. The noise of it filled up the hut and scared me.

Looking at the pile of sticks by the little stove, I decided to go outside and gather more. When I opened the door, I was surprised to see snow whirling down from the sky. It lay like gauze on the brown leaves curled at my feet and closed in around the hut like a thick white curtain. The wind-driven flakes stung my face and bare legs as I searched the ground for dead wood.

When I had an armful, I went back inside. Stuart was asleep, so I put the pile down quietly. "Guess what?" I whispered to Elizabeth. "It's snowing like mad."

Pressing our faces against one of the little windows, we watched the snow fall. The flakes whirled through the air so thickly we could barely see the trees surrounding the hut.

"Maybe it's a blizzard," Elizabeth said softly, "and we'll be stranded here."

Around noon, we made soup and practically forced Stuart to eat it. After he'd finished, he picked up a book, but the effort of holding it tired him out, so Elizabeth offered to read it to him.

He smiled at her. "That's something Gordy can't do," he said. "He hates to read."

Stuart handed Elizabeth an old high school literature book. "I've had it since twelfth grade," he said as she looked at the faded blue-and-gray cover. "Read me some poetry. There's one in there I like a lot. 'The Man He Killed,' by Thomas Hardy."

Elizabeth checked the table of contents, then turned to a page near the back of the book and began to read:

> Had he and I but met
> By some old ancient inn,
> We should have sat us down to wet
> Right many a nipperkin!

Elizabeth stumbled on "nipperkin" and giggled. " 'Wet right many a nipperkin'? What does *that* mean?"

"Drink a mug of beer," Stuart said, "a half-pint like in England."

That made us both laugh, but Stuart asked Elizabeth to go on with the poem. "It's not funny," he said.

Trying hard to stop giggling, Elizabeth read the rest. Stuart was right. It was a sad poem about a soldier who killed a man he might have been friends with if he hadn't been his enemy in a war.

"That's what war does to people," Stuart said. "Turns them into killers."

"But if Thomas Hardy hadn't killed that man, the man would've killed him," Elizabeth said. "They both shot at each other. It says so right here." She stabbed at a line of verse with her index finger and frowned.

Stuart leaned toward Elizabeth and me. He looked very earnest. "But suppose they hadn't?" he asked. "Suppose they'd thrown their guns down and said, 'This war is really dumb. Let's go get a beer.' "

Elizabeth shook her head. "Stuart, I just don't think that would happen."

"You never know till you try," Stuart said.

"Should I read some more poems?" Elizabeth asked.

Stuart coughed and shook his head. "No," he mumbled, "I think I'll take another nap."

He closed his eyes, and Elizabeth and I sat quietly, watching him sleep. Cautiously, Elizabeth leaned over and laid her palm against his forehead. Turning to me she said, "He's just burning up, Margaret. I think he's got a high fever."

From outside, we heard Gordy yelling something at Doug. The door of the hut opened, and Gordy stopped on the threshold with Doug and Toad behind him. At the sight of us huddled beside Stuart, they shut the door quietly, keeping out the snow gusting in behind them.

"Stuart's really sick," Elizabeth whispered.

Gordy bent over the cot, and Stuart opened his eyes. "They're my angels of the battlefield," he said, pointing at Elizabeth and me. "Don't know what I'd do without them."

Stuart's voice was raspy, and his eyes were even more fever bright. When he started coughing, Gordy brushed past Elizabeth and bent over him. "You're worse," he said.

"No, no," Stuart said. "The angels make me better. Their wings are so white and they sing so sweet. Don't worry, don't worry. Stay out of the street, don't make the old man mad, don't let him see you." His voice was barely a whisper. "Just the angels, that's all we need, the angels. You'll see after the war, after the war is over, after they've all gone home."

Stuart closed his eyes, and Gordy looked at Elizabeth. "What's the matter with him? What's he talking about?"

Elizabeth shook her head. "I think he's delirious because of the fever."

My heart sped up again. Delirious—I'd read books where people were delirious from fever. I remembered Little Eva's death in *Uncle Tom's Cabin*. She'd seen the angels coming down from heaven. Suppose Stuart was about to die? I started crying, I couldn't help it.

"Shut up, Magpie!" Gordy turned on me then. His face was dead white, and his voice was tight from all the anger squeezed into it. "We don't need no crybabies making things worse!"

"I'm so cold," Stuart muttered, "so cold. Isn't the war over yet? I want to go home, I want Mom, but the old man is there, he won't go away. Why can't it all be over?"

He struggled to sit up, but Gordy pushed him back down. "Just lie still," he said. "Lie still, Stuart, and get better. Please get better."

Stuart didn't seem to hear Gordy. "Have to go home,"

he said. "Can't kill, can't do it, don't want to see it. Wrong, all wrong, must be something I can do. Make the shooting stop, make it stop!"

"Stuart, it's me," Gordy said. He tried to keep him from getting up, but Stuart was fighting him. "Help me," he yelled to Doug and Toad.

They grabbed Stuart's shoulders and shoved him down, but as he fell back, he kicked out hard and sent his literature book flying. Elizabeth picked it up and clasped it against her chest. I was scared. From the way Stuart was acting, you would have thought we were his enemies, not his friends.

In the midst of all the turmoil, Stuart started coughing so hard he couldn't struggle anymore. He coughed till he could hardly breathe and then he lay still. Slowly his eyes traveled from face to face, studying each one of us. The tension went out of him, and he closed his eyes.

"Is he asleep?" Elizabeth whispered.

Gordy leaned over his brother and stared at him. He nodded. Then he motioned us to follow him outside.

The ground was white now, and the snow was still falling thick and fast, closing around us like a cloak. From its perch on a limb high overhead, a crow cawed once and then lifted itself into the air. I watched it fly away, its shape blurred by the falling snow.

"Stuart needs a doctor," Elizabeth said. Her words came out in angry puffs of white smoke.

"Did I ask you to butt your nose in my business?" Gordy asked. "When I want your opinion, I'll ask for it, Lizard."

"She's right, Gordy," Doug said. "He can't stay here. He's getting sicker and sicker."

"Suppose he busts out of there and tries to go home?" Toad asked. "Your old man will kill him."

"What do you think the army will do to him?" Gordy had tears in his eyes. "Give him a medal for deserting?"

"We have to do something!" Elizabeth yelled. "We can't just let him die!"

The five of us stood there, staring at each other. The snow swirled around us as if it were never going to stop, blotting out the tops of the trees and drifting against the hut. Elizabeth's words lingered in the air, but no one spoke.

If only I really were an angel of the battlefield, I thought, I'd make the war stop. I'd make it safe for Stuart to go home, I'd make it safe for Jimmy and Joe, too. I'd make it safe for all the little children in the world and their mothers and their fathers and their grandparents.

But I wasn't an angel of the battlefield, and neither was Elizabeth. I didn't know what to do. And neither did anybody else.

17

Standing in the snow, cold and miserable, we stared at each other, waiting for somebody to come up with a plan. As the silence grew and no one spoke, I found myself thinking of a solution. I turned it this way and that, examining it from all angles till I was sure it would work. The problem was saying it out loud. I wasn't very good at speaking up. Suppose they laughed at me? Gordy would scoff at anything I said, I was sure of it. Nudging Elizabeth, I forced myself to speak. "Why don't we ask Barbara to help?"

"Barbara?" Gordy stared at me.

"We need someone grown-up," I said, feeling my face grow hot with embarrassment. I wasn't used to thinking of things for other people to do. "We can't tell our parents about Stuart. They wouldn't understand. But Barbara would."

"Her husband died in the war, you dope," Gordy said. "She's not going to have any sympathy for Stuart."

"She likes him," I said. "She even likes you."

Gordy's face got red, and Doug laughed.

"You must be out of your mind, Magpie. Nobody likes the Smiths," Toad said. "Except me and Doug," he added quickly when Gordy glared at him.

Suddenly, Elizabeth turned to Gordy and said, "I think

it's a good idea. Barbara's not like our parents. We can trust her, I know we can."

Gordy scowled at Elizabeth. "What can she do that we can't?" he wanted to know.

"For one thing, she can take Stuart to the doctor," I said, surprising myself. It was the first time I'd ever dared speak up to Gordy, but if I couldn't persuade him I was right, Stuart would die. I wasn't going to let that happen.

"Barbara has a driver's license," I went on, "and we don't. How else is he going to get anywhere? He's too sick to walk. She can drive him."

Gordy thought about what I'd said, looking for flaws in my plan. "Suppose she does do it, just suppose," he muttered, "and the doctor turns him in?"

"He doesn't have to know Stuart's a deserter," I said. "We'll go to a doctor who doesn't know any of us, we'll give a false name, say Stuart's in high school. The doctor will just think he's sick."

Doug nodded. "Don't doctors take some kind of oath that says they have to heal everybody, no matter what?"

"That's right," I said. "Elizabeth and I can go to Barbara's house now and ask her. Okay?" I stared at Gordy, waiting for him to answer.

Gordy looked at Doug and Toad. They didn't say anything at first. I guess they were used to Gordy being the boss. Finally, Toad said, "Let them try. Stuart needs help, Gordy."

Doug stared at the falling snow. "Toad's right," he muttered. "We can't take care of him anymore."

Gordy glared at Elizabeth and me. "Well, go on," he yelled. "Ask Barbara. What are you waiting for?" Then he turned his back on us and went into the hut. Silently, Doug and Toad followed him.

As soon as the door shut behind the boys, Elizabeth and I ran through the woods toward home. The ground was slippery, and the wind whirled the snow in our faces, almost blinding us. By the time we crossed the train tracks, my feet felt like lumps of ice. Elizabeth's hair was frosted white, and snow clung to her eyelashes. She looked like the queen of winter.

"First we go inside so our mothers will think we're just getting home from school," Elizabeth said. "Then we change our clothes and go to Barbara's house."

She dashed home, and I tore across the yard and up the back steps. When I burst into the kitchen, stamping snow off my feet, Mother wasn't pleased. I was sure to catch my death, she said. But, after making sure I was swaddled in mittens and scarves and boots and extra socks, she begrudgingly let me go outside to play in the snow.

"School's closed tomorrow," Elizabeth told me gleefully as I stumped down the sidewalk toward her. "Mother heard it on the radio. We're supposed to get at least seven or eight inches of snow before it stops. And Christmas vacation starts Wednesday. That gives us a whole extra day not to worry about Mrs. Hitler."

All the way to Barbara's big brick house on Beech Drive, I found myself looking for Gordy. Usually he took the fun out of days like this by ambushing us with snowballs packed hard as rocks. But not today. He was down in the woods with Stuart, and we were safe.

Kids were already sled riding on Beech Drive. As we started down the hill, Frankie and Bruce whizzed past and yelled at us to join them, but Elizabeth and I shook our heads and trudged into Barbara's yard. Luckily for us, she was just coming around the corner of her house, pulling Brent on a little sled.

Barbara smiled when she saw us. "You must think I'm crazy, dragging a baby out in a snowstorm, but this is his first one. I wanted him to see it."

Flanked by Elizabeth and me, Barbara pulled the sled out of the yard and down the street. All around us the snow tumbled down in flakes as big as duck feathers. When I tilted my head back and looked at the sky, I felt dizzy. It was like being trapped inside a glass paperweight shaken by a giant.

After we'd walked a block or so, I looked at Barbara. Her face was as rosy as Elizabeth's, and her eyelashes sparkled with snow. I could remember watching her skin the cat on the jungle gym and wondering if I'd ever be as big and strong as she was. She'd worn her hair in long, thick braids then, like I wore mine now. Surely we could trust Barbara.

Taking a deep breath, I looked up into her smiling face. "Do you remember Stuart Smith?" I asked her.

"Oh, Margaret," Barbara whispered, her eyes wide with alarm. "Don't tell me. He's not hurt—or . . . ? Nothing's happened to Stu, not this close to Christmas?"

I shook my head, and, under a casing of snow, my braids hit my cheeks with the sting of frozen rope. "You like Stuart, don't you?"

"Of course." Barbara stared at me. "Are you sure he's all right, Margaret?"

While I tried to think of the best way to tell her the

truth about Stuart, Barbara said, "It was bad enough to lose Butch. Now it seems like every day someone else I went to school with dies. I can't stand much more." Tears brimmed in her eyes, and she wiped them away with the back of her mittened hand.

I glanced at Elizabeth, hoping she might butt in and say something, but she just bit her lower lip and kicked at the snow as we walked along. It was up to me.

"What if I told you Stuart deserted?" I asked. "Would you turn him in?"

Barbara stopped so suddenly the sled bumped her heels and Brent almost fell off. She looked at me, then at Elizabeth. All around us the snow fell, covering bushes and trees and roofs, softening the edges of houses, blending streets and lawns and sky together so you could hardly see where one thing ended and something else began.

"Where is he?" Barbara whispered.

"First you have to promise not to tell anyone," I said.

"Not a single living soul," Elizabeth added.

"You can tell me," Barbara said. "I'd never betray Stuart, no matter what he's done."

"He's down in the woods across the train tracks," I told her. "Gordy's been hiding him since last summer."

"And he's sick," Elizabeth said. "Really sick."

"We're afraid he's going to die." As soon as I said it, I started to cry.

For a moment Barbara didn't speak. She stood motionless in the falling snow. "What can I do to help?" she asked at last.

"He needs a doctor," I said.

"And you know how to drive," Elizabeth said. "You can take him to one."

"Will you do it?" I asked her. "Please? Stuart doesn't believe in wars and killing. Even if the army caught him, he wouldn't shoot anybody. He said so."

"Gordy thinks you won't help him." Elizabeth tugged at Barbara's sleeve to get her attention. "He says you'll hate Stuart for deserting because Butch got killed."

Barbara shook her head. "Hate Stuart? No," she said slowly. "We've been friends since we were in kindergarten. Once I actually beat up Donald because he made Stu cry. He was such a bully, I hated him, but Stu was like a brother to me."

She bent down to retrieve a mitten Brent had thrown into the snow. "I guess I'm not surprised Stu deserted," she said. "Some people just aren't meant to be soldiers."

"Will you help us, then?" I asked.

Barbara stuck Brent's hand back into his mitten and straightened up. "Show me where he is," she said. "I'll do whatever I can."

Hurrying through the snow, we led her across the train tracks and took turns pulling Brent's sled through the woods. When we finally reached the clearing, Barbara was out of breath, and Brent was whimpering. She scooped him up into her arms and stared at the hut. Never had it looked more desolate. Dusk was graying the snow, and the wind rattled the treetops. Shivering, we followed Barbara to the door.

18

When we came inside, stamping off snow, Gordy scowled at all of us, but Stuart didn't move. He lay still, his eyes closed.

Handing Brent to me, Barbara knelt beside Stuart. Laying a hand on his forehead, she winced as if his flesh had burned her.

At the touch of her hand, Stuart woke up. Reaching toward her, he brushed her face with his fingertips as if he couldn't believe his eyes. "Barb, is it really you?" he asked hoarsely. "What are you doing here?'"

"Stu," she whispered. "Oh, Stu, what kind of a mess have you gotten yourself into?"

"Something even you can't get me out of, Barb," he murmured.

Barbara seized both his hands and held them tightly. "How long have you been sick?" she asked.

"Don't know," he mumbled. "Forever, I think. Can't remember where or when."

Barbara turned to Gordy as Stuart closed his eyes again. "When did this start?"

"He had a cold, a cough, that's all," Gordy said. "Then it got lots worse a few days ago. We been taking care of him. Even Lizard and Magpie. But he just keeps getting worse."

"Can you stay with him tonight and keep him warm?" Barbara asked.

Gordy shrugged. "Yeah, sure. I guess so."

"I'll call a doctor tomorrow and borrow Dad's car, but you'll have to get him to Calvert Road. Can you do that?"

"He's too weak to walk that far," Gordy said.

"I'll bring Jimmy's bobsled," I said. "We can pull him through the woods on it."

"Meet me at ten-thirty tomorrow morning," Barbara said. "Just across the train tracks. Give him more aspirin tonight, and make sure he drinks lots of water. Melt snow if you have to."

Bending over Stuart, Barbara kissed his forehead. "Don't you dare get any worse, Stuart Smith," she whispered.

He stared up at her, frowning as if he'd just thought of something. "Don't tell anybody where I am," he said. "Don't tell my mother or the old man. Nobody must know. Secret."

"I promise, Stu," Barbara said. "I won't say a word. Just rest, okay? I'll see you tomorrow."

Outside, the snow was still falling. Big flakes blew in my face, chilling my forehead till it ached. My nose ran, my toes and fingers hurt, my leg muscles ached with weariness. It was almost dark, and Brent was fussing. Barbara carried him, and I pulled the sled.

"What's wrong with him?" Elizabeth asked Barbara.

"It's probably pneumonia," Barbara said.

"Do you think he'll be all right?" I asked. We were crossing the train tracks, and I was having trouble yanking the sled over the rails. When Barbara didn't answer, I looked at her. She was frowning.

"I hope so," she said at last. Hugging Brent, Barbara took the sled from me. After scrambling up the slippery bank to the road, she turned to look back at Elizabeth and me. "You two better go home," she said. "It must be past five."

*

I was worried my parents would punish me for coming home so late, but when I slipped into the house they were sitting at the kitchen table reading the *Evening Star.* They were both too absorbed in the war news to notice my wet clothes or the time. A pot of stew simmered on the stove, and the windows were so steamy you couldn't see the snow whirling down outside. Except for the noise of the stew bubbling and the clock ticking, the room was silent, too silent.

"What's wrong?" A lump filled my throat as they turned to me, and my knees went suddenly weak. "Has something happened?"

Daddy shook his head and shoved the newspaper away. "The Nazis are hitting us with everything they've got. It looks bad for Jimmy." Shoving his chair back, he grabbed his jacket from the hook by the door.

"Walt," Mother said. "Don't go out now. Dinner's ready."

"You and Margaret go ahead and eat," Daddy said. "I'm not hungry."

A swirl of windblown snow eddied in the doorway. Then Daddy was gone.

"Where's he going?" I turned to Mother.

126

"Don't worry about him," Mother said. "He needs some thinking time, that's all." She went to the door and pushed the window curtain aside. Peering out into the white darkness, she stood quietly for a few seconds.

"Get those wet shoes off," she said without looking at me, "and sit down."

Going to the stove, she ladled stew onto our plates, and we sat down to eat. Although I didn't want to think about the war, I couldn't keep my eyes from the newspaper Daddy had left on the table. "Heavy casualties," it said. "High death toll for Allies."

Poking at the meat on my plate, I remembered the day Jimmy left for the war, tall and thin and freckled like me, but suddenly grown-up, a stranger in his uniform, hugging us all, swinging me off the ground. "Be a good girl, Maggie May," he'd said. "Keep on stepping on those cracks till you break Hitler's back."

Then he'd picked up his duffle bag and gotten on the train. We stood on the platform, Mother, Daddy, and I. Smoke plumed up into the sky from the engine, and steam hissed out in a cloud from under the wheels. The train began to move, slowly at first, its pistons pumping louder and harder as it picked up speed. The whistle blew, a long, loud blast that hurt my ears, and we waved to Jimmy as his car passed.

The car windows were open, and the soldiers leaned out, waving and waving, their good-byes drowned out by the whistle and the chug, chug, chug of the locomotive pulling them out of sight. Then the train was gone. Our family and all the other families walked slowly home.

Poking at my stew, I gazed at the steamy kitchen window and thought about the funny pictures Jimmy used to draw on the wet surface. Dogs smoking pipes, fish taking walks, mice chasing cats. The next morning you could still see the lines on the glass, ghosts of dogs and fish and mice, which made Mother sigh and shake her head.

In those days, Jimmy roughhoused with Joe Crawford and played football, carried me piggyback all over College Hill and called me silly names like Princess Pea. Now he was far away in a forest whose name I couldn't pronounce, and enemy soldiers were shooting at him.

Oh, why hadn't my brother stayed home like Stuart? I could have hidden him in the woods and taken care of him. Joe, too. They wouldn't have gotten sick, either, Elizabeth and I wouldn't have let them.

"Margaret, eat your dinner." Mother was looking at me and frowning. "It's a sin to waste food."

To make her happy, I choked down the rest of my stew. As she took my empty plate, I looked up at Mother. "You don't think anything has happened to Jimmy, do you?"

A tear rolled down her cheek, and she brushed it away. It was the first time I'd ever seen her cry. The sight of that tear scared me more than the big black headlines on the front page.

"Just pray for him," she whispered. "Pray for him and all our boys."

"Don't you wish Jimmy hadn't been drafted?" I asked her. "Don't you wish he was right here?"

Mother wiped her eyes with a corner of her apron and stared at me. "What a thing to say, Margaret. It was Jimmy's duty to go to war. As an American, he had no choice but to fight for his country."

I looked at her for a moment. Her face was set, her voice was sure. She had no doubts. When war came, you fought. You had no choice.

I couldn't tell her what Stuart believed. She wouldn't understand.

Silently, I helped clear the table. As we filled the sink with hot water, we heard Daddy on the back porch, stamping the snow off his feet. "What a night," he said. "The snow is coming down like it's never going to stop."

"Do you want your dinner now?" Mother asked. "I kept it hot for you."

Daddy shook his head and went into the living room. Turning on the radio, he sank down in his armchair to listen to H. V. Kaltenborn talk about the war. Tonight his deep voice was scarier than the Shadow's. The evil he was talking about was real. To avoid hearing him, I ran up to my room and shut my door.

Outside the warmth of our house, the snow fell thicker and harder than ever. Pressing my nose against the window, I watched the big flakes swirl to earth in the funnel of light from a street lamp. Barely visible, Mr. Zimmerman walked Major past our house. The dog leapt ahead, bounding in and out of snow, but Mr. Zimmerman moved slowly, cautiously, as if he were afraid of falling.

As I got into bed, a train blew its whistle, reminding me of Stuart down in the woods, cold and sick, with no one but Gordy to keep him safe. Even worse, somewhere across the ocean, Jimmy crouched in a foxhole. Maybe it was snowing there too, but mixed with the white flakes were bombs and bullets. Men were hurt and dying, lying in the snow, turning it red with their blood. Men who might have been friends if they hadn't had to shoot at each other.

Closing my eyes, I huddled into a ball under my covers and tried to think of something else. The war ending. Jimmy and Joe coming home. Everything being the way it used to be.

But how was that? The war had lasted so long I couldn't remember a time when people didn't hate the Japanese and the Nazis. Had there really been days when we could have all the sugar and butter we wanted, when nothing was rationed, when no bombs fell anywhere?

19

The next morning I woke up with the sun shining in my eyes. College Hill was sparkling white, buried under nine inches of snow. It wouldn't last long, a couple of days maybe, and then the temperature would rise and melt it all away, but this morning the thermometer on our back porch said it was only eighteen degrees. The wind was blowing, sending snow flying across the yard, making it even colder.

"Where do you think you're going?" Mother asked when she saw me struggling to pull my boots over my shoes.

"Coasting on Beech Drive," I said, careful to keep my head lowered so she wouldn't see my face and know I was lying. "I promised Elizabeth I'd bring the bobsled. All the kids are going to be there."

"You know how easily you get sick," Mother said. "One more strep throat, and Dr. Brinkley will have your tonsils out."

"I'll be okay," I said. "Mrs. Katz always invites us in for hot chocolate."

"What's in that bag?" Mother pointed at a paper sack I'd filled with Jimmy's old clothes. Stuart couldn't go to the doctor in the rags of his uniform, so I'd borrowed a few things for him. I was sure Jimmy wouldn't mind. Like Barbara, he'd understand about Stuart.

131

"It's some spare clothes," I said. "In case I get wet. I can change at Judy's." Ashamed to look at Mother, I zipped my jacket. Never had I told so many lies. I felt bad and wicked, but saving Stuart's life was more important than telling my mother the truth.

"That's very sensible," Mother said, making me feel even worse.

Without meeting her eyes, I ran out the back door and down the steps. After pulling the bobsled out from under the porch, I plowed through the snow to Elizabeth's house.

Mrs. Crawford opened the door and stared at me. "You and Elizabeth," she said. "What a pair. Why anyone would want to leave a nice, warm house on a day like this is beyond me."

Elizabeth squeezed around her mother. The layers of clothes she wore made her look as if she'd gained twenty pounds overnight.

With the bobsled bouncing at our heels, we ran down the alley, crossed the train tracks, and headed for the woods. Gordy was waiting for us outside the hut, pacing back and forth, trampling down the snow.

"Where have you dopes been?" he asked. "It's almost ten o'clock."

Ignoring Gordy, we pushed past him. Inside the hut, Elizabeth peeled off several layers of Joe's clothes, and I pulled things out of my bag, including a razor and a pair of scissors. By the time he was shaved and dressed in Jimmy's and Joe's sweaters and jeans, Stuart looked like a high school student, someone much too young to be a soldier.

The only bad thing was his hair. None of us knew a

thing about barbering, but Elizabeth insisted he couldn't go anywhere till it was cut. When she finished hacking at it, Stuart's hair looked like badly mowed grass.

"I guess there's more to being a barber than I thought," Elizabeth admitted as we all stared glumly at Stuart. "But at least he doesn't look like the crazy man from the experimental farm anymore," she added. "Just some poor guy who let his mother cut his hair."

Flushed with fever and unsteady on his feet, Stuart followed us outside and collapsed on the bobsled. The effort made him cough.

"Angels," he murmured as Elizabeth and I covered him with blankets. "Angels guard my sled at night."

Gordy grabbed the rope and began to pull. It was hard work. The ground was uneven, and the snow hid roots and rocks, making the sled bounce and jolt. To help, Elizabeth pushed, and I tried to steady Stuart. We could have used Toad and Doug, but they hadn't shown up, and we couldn't wait for them.

By the time we reached Calvert Road, we were all exhausted.

"Where's Barbara?" Gordy stared down the snowy stretch of road. Tire tracks made zigzag patterns on the white surface, but there was no sign of a car. Overhead a crow cawed, and the wind blew snow in our faces, making Stuart cough.

Just when we were about to give up hope, we saw a black Plymouth coming slowly toward us. As it drew nearer, we recognized Barbara at the wheel. A few feet away from us, she braked, the car slid a little, the tire chains bit into the snow, and she stopped.

Telling me to hold Brent, Barbara ran to the sled. With

Gordy's help, she got Stuart on his feet and maneuvered him into the back seat. Stuart didn't seem to know what was going on, but he curled up with his head in Elizabeth's lap and fell asleep.

After hiding the bobsled in the woods, Gordy climbed in with Stuart and Elizabeth, and I sat in the front seat. Brent crowed with delight when Barbara stepped on the gas and we slid sideways. Clutching Brent, I watched Barbara struggle to point the car in the right direction. Slowly we inched forward, and I relaxed a little.

"Daddy almost didn't let me go," Barbara said. "I told him Brent was due for his checkup, and he wanted to drive us to the doctor himself. I insisted I could do it, but I'm scared to death. My leg's shaking so hard I can hardly keep my foot on the gas pedal. I never drove in snow before."

"Want me to take over?" Gordy leaned toward her. "I know how. Donald taught me."

Barbara gripped the steering wheel tighter and shook her head. "No, I'm okay," she said. "I can do it."

While we slipped and slid slowly down Calvert Road, Stuart got the idea we were on our way to a basketball game.

"We'll beat those Mustangs," he said. "Nothing can stop the Hawks." Then he sang the Hyattsdale High fight song, but he started coughing and had to stop halfway through.

"What doctor are you taking him to?" Gordy asked Barbara.

"Dr. Deitz," she said. "I picked his name out of the phone book. He doesn't know me, and I don't know him. I told the nurse that Stu was my brother. Everything will be all right, Gordy. Nobody's going to ask any questions."

"How are we going to pay him?" Gordy asked. I could tell he didn't trust Barbara any more than he trusted Elizabeth and me. He was sure something would go wrong.

"I've got money," Barbara said. "Stop worrying."

Gordy slumped down beside Stuart. "Did you hear what Barbara said?" he asked. "You're supposed to be her brother. Don't say nothing about the army or living in the woods or not wanting to kill anybody, okay? Just let the doctor look at you and keep your mouth shut."

"If I'm Barbara's brother," Stuart said, "what's my name supposed to be?"

"Smith, just like it really is," Barbara said. "That's what I told the nurse my name was."

"Smith, Barbara Smith," Stuart said slowly. He wasn't looking at her. His head was turned to the side, and he was watching the snowy landscape glide by outside. "What a nice name. I like the sound of it. Barbara Smith, Barbara Smith."

"How about us?" Elizabeth asked. "Are we in the family, too?"

"Oh, no," Gordy muttered when Barbara nodded. "Lizard and Magpie Smith—if they're supposed to be my sisters, I'm not going in that doctor's office. I'll wait in the car."

By the time Barbara parked in front of Dr. Deitz's office on Farragut Street, Gordy had calmed down, but Stuart was still confused. We had to persuade him to get out of the car and then help him to the door. He was pretty tottery, and we kept reminding him what he was supposed to tell the doctor.

"Is he going to send me to war?" Stuart asked.

"Not if you keep quiet," Gordy said. From the way he was scowling at Stuart, I had a feeling Gordy wanted to punch him. "Sometimes I think the old man socked your brains out your ears," he muttered as he opened the door.

The nurse looked up when we came in, half dragging Stuart and tracking snow all over the floor. She wasn't pleased at the mess we were making, but she told us to take a seat. "Dr. Deitz will see your brother in a couple of minutes, Miss Smith," she added as Barbara wrote her name on the sign-in sheet.

The nurse looked at Gordy, Elizabeth, and me. I was holding Brent, who was yanking on one of my braids and laughing.

"These are my brothers and sisters," Barbara said. "My parents are at work today, so I had to bring all the kids with me."

The nurse took Stuart's arm and led him out of the waiting room. We watched the door close behind him before we sat down.

The office was very quiet. Apparently, we were the only people either sick or brave enough to venture out on the snowy roads. Except for Brent's baby babble, no one spoke. We sat in the pine-paneled room on the hard black couches like strangers waiting for a bus.

On a low table near me was a pile of *Life* magazines. General Charles de Gaulle, the French army leader, stared at me from a November cover. Other issues showed soldiers, fighter planes, German prisoners of war, and battleships—war scene after war scene, going on and on and on as endlessly as the war itself.

Gordy pulled a magazine out of the stack and started leafing through it, stopping to look at pictures of dead soldiers and exploding bombs and crashing planes. Staring at him, I noticed how dirty the back of his neck was. Close up, his skin was gray, and his body had a stale, unpleasant odor.

As I edged away from Gordy, Barbara leaned toward me to take Brent, and I handed him over gladly. His bottom was damp, and my temple hurt from all the yanks on my braids. For a baby, he was amazingly strong.

Turning back to Gordy, I said, "Aren't your parents going to be mad because you didn't come home last night?"

"What's it to you, Magpie?" Gordy scowled at me and went on flipping through *Life*. Pausing at a picture of a bomber, he said, "That's a Heinkel 111. Donald's shot a lot of them right out of the sky." He pointed a finger at me and made a series of exploding sounds.

Elizabeth and Barbara looked at Gordy, and Brent tried to imitate the noise he'd made. "What did you tell your parents, Gordy?" Barbara asked.

Keeping his eyes focused on a photograph of gaunt soldiers trudging through a wasteland of rubble and bomb craters, Gordy shrugged. "I didn't tell them anything," he mumbled. "The line was busy."

That was Gordy's idea of a joke, I guessed. There wasn't any telephone in the hut.

"You mean you just didn't go home?" Elizabeth stared at Gordy. "Aren't you scared your old man will beat you?"

Gordy flashed Elizabeth a look of contempt. "Mind your own beeswax, Lizard."

As Barbara opened her mouth to speak, Dr. Deitz walked toward us, supporting Stuart with a firm hand under his elbow. At the sight of his stiff white coat, the stethoscope around his neck, and his shiny black shoes, we all stopped talking. I prayed Stuart hadn't said anything to give himself away.

"Your brother has pneumonia. He's a very sick young man," Dr. Deitz began. "I can't understand why you waited so long to bring him to me."

While the doctor spoke, Stuart sank down on the couch beside Barbara. He looked too tired to hold his head up.

"My parents don't have much money," Barbara said. "They were hoping he'd get well on his own, but he keeps getting worse."

Dr. Deitz nodded. His eyes moved back and forth, scanning us. He seemed puzzled, probably because we didn't look like a family. "He needs to be hospitalized," he told Barbara.

She shook her head. "We can't afford it."

"Just give him medicine or something," Gordy said. "He'll be okay."

"I can write a prescription," Dr. Deitz told Gordy, "but pneumonia isn't something to take lightly. Stuart needs to be taken care of, nursed."

"We can do that ourselves," Gordy said, his face reddening. From the way he was glaring at the doctor, I was worried Gordy might start swearing or something.

"It's in his best interest to go to the hospital," Dr. Deitz said, but Barbara shook her head.

"We can't pay for it," she repeated. "It's out of the question."

Elizabeth and I looked at each other. In a hospital, someone would be sure to discover Stuart was a deserter. He'd be sent back to the army, and then, as soon as he was well enough, he'd have to go to war.

Dr. Deitz sighed, "I can't legally force you to put this young man in a hospital," he said as he wrote out a prescription, "but I think you're making a big mistake."

Handing Barbara the prescription, he added, "Keep him warm. Make sure he stays in bed and drinks lots of liquid. Give him broth, soup, something nourishing but easy to digest."

Frowning, he watched Barbara pay the receptionist. He was still frowning when we left.

After we all got into the car, Barbara gripped the steering wheel. Tears rolled down her cheeks. "What are we going to do now?"

"Just get the medicine," Stuart mumbled. "Don't worry, I'll be okay. Gordy and I can manage."

Barbara shook her head and turned around to look at him. "You can't stay in that hut, Stu. It's too cold and damp."

When Stuart just shrugged and closed his eyes, Barbara stared at him, her forehead wrinkled with worry.

"Just leave us be, will you?" Gordy leaned forward, his face inches from Barbara's. "The Smiths take care of their own problems. We don't need help from anybody, including you!"

"Gordy," Stuart murmured drowsily, "don't talk like that. Not to Barbara."

Gordy muttered something that sounded pretty nasty and turned his head away. A gust of wind shook the car, and I looked through the windshield at the white lawns and streets of Hyattsdale. While we'd been in the doctor's office, the snowplow had come through.

Two little girls passed by, towing a younger child on a sled. Their cheeks were red, and they were laughing, but no one laughed in the Plymouth. We just sat quietly, waiting for someone to think of a way out of our predicament. We'd told Barbara about Stuart, she'd helped just like I thought she would, but we still didn't know what to do.

20

*L*ike yesterday, the silence went on and on as we all struggled to come up with an idea. This time it was Barbara who spoke first. "I have a suggestion," she said slowly.

We all looked at her, hoping she'd thought of the perfect solution.

"We can take him to my house," she said.

"Your house?" Elizabeth and I spoke together as if it were a line we'd been practicing for a play.

"Are you crazy?" Gordy stared at her. "Your parents aren't going to want a deserter in their house. They'll turn him in quicker than this." He snapped his fingers hard right in Barbara's face, but she didn't even flinch.

"You don't know my mother," Barbara said. "She's got the biggest heart in the world. She can't even turn a stray cat away. One look at Stu and she'll have him tucked up in bed, safe and warm."

Stuart gazed at Barbara with a sort of sad, dreamy expression on his face, but he didn't say anything. Even with blankets mounded over him, he shivered as a gust of wind rocked the car.

"What about your old man?" Gordy asked. "I bet he gets rid of those stray cats fast enough."

"Believe me," Barbara said, "in our house, Dad does what Mother tells him to do."

While Gordy muttered something about henpecked husbands, Elizabeth said, "But it's against the law to help a deserter. Your parents could go to jail if anybody finds out about Stuart."

Barbara thought for a moment. "My parents don't have to know he's AWOL, do they? I'll just tell them Stuart's sick and he needs somebody to take care of him. They know about his, his—" Her voice trailed off, and she fiddled with the controls for the heater. "They'll understand," she muttered.

"Why don't you say what you mean?" Gordy leaned across the seat and glowered at Barbara. "I know how this whole stupid town feels about my family."

Gordy was yelling at Barbara, his face red with anger, and she shrank back from him, shaking her head. "My parents like Stuart," she said. "They always have. He's not—" Stopping again in midsentence, Barbara gripped the steering wheel and stared straight ahead at the snowy street. Her face was red, too.

"Not like the rest of us," Gordy finished. "Not poor white trash like me and Donald and Junie and Ernest and Victor." He slumped back in the seat and folded his arms across his chest.

Stuart turned toward Gordy, frowning, then looked at Barbara. His eyes glittered, his face was flushed, and he seemed to be struggling to stay awake. "Always fighting," he murmured. " 'I shot at him as he at me, and killed him in his place. I shot him dead because—' " Stuart's voice faltered and he coughed.

"Talk sense!" Gordy punched Stuart's arm, and Elizabeth glared at him.

"Leave him alone," she said. "It's from that poem, 'The Man He Killed.' If you weren't so dumb you'd know poetry when you heard it."

Stuart tried to smile at Elizabeth, but he was coughing too hard.

Barbara leaned over the seat and stared at him. "Stu," she said softly, trying to get his attention. "What do you think? Should I take you home with me?"

Stuart nodded and tried to focus on Barbara. "If you think it's okay. I don't want to get anyone in trouble." He coughed again. "Especially you."

Gordy rolled his eyes and groaned. "Don't be such a jerk, Stuart. Her old man will get on the phone and call the army the minute he sees you. I swear you've got rocks in your head."

Stuart shrugged. "Then I'll die in the war," he said, "but if I stay in the woods, I'll die too."

Ignoring us all, Barbara started the car and drove slowly back to College Hill. When she got to Calvert Road, she stopped where she'd picked us up. "You three better get out here," she said to Elizabeth, Gordy, and me.

Elizabeth and I slid out of the warm car into the cold wind, but Gordy stayed where he was. Glaring at Barbara, he said, "My brother doesn't go anywhere without me."

"Try to understand, Gordy," Barbara said, "you've done a lot for Stu, but you can't help him now. Let me talk to my parents first. You can come to my house later this afternoon and see him."

"Do what Barbara says, Gordy," Stuart said. "You can trust her, honest you can."

Gordy frowned at his brother, but he got out of the car.

143

The three of us watched Barbara drive away. Gordy pulled the sled out of its hiding place, and we started walking up Calvert Road toward home. The wind blew hard in our faces, stinging tears from our eyes, and the snow, packed down by the plow, was slippery under our feet.

Two or three cars passed us, and, at the sight of one, an old black Ford, Gordy stopped. Muttering a couple of curse words, he ducked behind Elizabeth and me, but he wasn't fast enough. Mrs. Smith and three or four little kids peered out the windows as the man grabbed Gordy.

"You dumb kid, where the hell have you been?" Mr. Smith yelled, shaking Gordy. "You think I got nothing better to do than waste gas looking for you? You had your mother worried to death."

While Elizabeth and I watched, Mr. Smith punched Gordy hard enough to knock him down. With blood spouting from his nose, Gordy scrambled to his feet only to be knocked down again.

"Stop it!" Elizabeth screamed. "Leave him alone!"

Mr. Smith looked at Elizabeth as if he hadn't noticed her before. Turning to Gordy, he sneered, "You got girls taking up for you now?"

Without waiting for an answer, he seized Gordy's arm and thrust him roughly into the back seat with the other kids. Sliding behind the steering wheel, Mr. Smith slammed the door and stepped on the gas. The tires spun for a couple of seconds against the icy snow, but then the old car leapt ahead, belching a cloud of exhaust into Elizabeth's and my faces. The last thing I saw was June's face pressed against the rear window as Mr. Smith drove away.

Elizabeth and I stared at each other. On the white snow

at our feet were drops of red—Gordy's blood. Over our heads, a blue jay screeched, and, not far away, a train whistle blew.

"Let's go home," Elizabeth said.

Wordlessly, we trudged toward the railroad tracks. The train whistle blew again, the lights at the crossing flashed, and the bell rang. Standing in the snow, we watched the engine approach, spewing smoke and cinders into the air. The big wheels shook the ground under our feet.

Deafened by the noise, we looked up and waved at the engineer. He grinned and waved back. Troop car after troop car rocked past, thundering toward the war, and we kept on waving, waving, and waving at the soldiers. Then came jeeps and tanks and big guns, hundreds of them, it seemed.

Finally the train disappeared down the track, leaving an acrid cloud of gray smoke behind. Cinders drifted down and blackened the snow around us, and we closed our eyes to keep them out.

"If I was Gordy, I'd run away," Elizabeth said as we dragged the sled across the tracks.

"Me, too."

I watched Elizabeth slip and slide over the snow toward her house. Then I walked around to our backyard and put the bobsled under the porch. It was the first time in my whole life I hadn't wanted to go coasting.

*

Later in the afternoon I was in my room reading *Anne of Green Gables* for the third time when I heard Elizabeth running up the steps. Dashing through my door, she said, "Let's go to Barbara's house and see if Stuart's okay."

Outside the sun cast long, blue shadows across the snow, and I shivered as a blast of wind rocked the branches over my head. By the time we reached Barbara's house, my nose felt as cold as a carrot stuck in a snowman's face. We hesitated on the porch, staring at the wreath of holly on the door, afraid to ring the bell. Suppose Barbara had been wrong about her mother and Stuart wasn't there?

If we hadn't heard footsteps behind us, we might have sneaked away. Whirling around, we saw Gordy trudging toward the house. His head was down, and he hadn't seen us yet. For the first time it occurred to me that his jacket was too small and too thin to keep him warm.

As he drew nearer, Gordy looked up. One eye was black and nearly swollen shut, but he managed to scowl at Elizabeth and me.

"What are you jerks doing here?" he said. "Can't I ever get away from you?"

"We came to see how Stuart is," Elizabeth said. We stood our ground, facing him. At any minute, I expected to feel his fist plow into my stomach, but Gordy just stood there, kicking at the snow and frowning.

"Did your father do that?" Elizabeth peered at Gordy's eye.

"No," Gordy said sarcastically, "I ran into a door."

"I hate your old man," Elizabeth said. "He ought to be locked up, the way he acts."

Ignoring her, Gordy pressed the bell. In a few seconds, the door opened, and a tall man with a pipe in his hand stared down at us.

"Mr. Fisher?" Elizabeth said.

Barbara's father nodded. "Elizabeth, Margaret, and Gordy," he said. "Right?"

It was our turn to nod. Standing aside, he ushered us into a hallway smelling of pipe smoke and fresh green pine. In the living room, Mrs. Fisher was hanging balls on a big tree. A fire crackled on the hearth, and Bing Crosby crooned "White Christmas" on the Victrola in the corner. For a moment I felt as if I'd stepped into the kind of movie that always has a happy ending.

Then Gordy said, "Where's my brother?" His loud voice shattered the spell of the Fishers' house.

"He's asleep, dear." Mrs. Fisher laid the box of ornaments on the coffee table and joined us in the hall. "Oh, my," she said, looking at Gordy's eye. "How did that happen?"

"His father hit him," Elizabeth said. "He socked him so hard he knocked him down and made his nose bleed, then he punched him again." Her voice rose, filling with admiration. "Gordy didn't even cry."

"She's lying," Gordy said. "My old man never laid a hand on me."

Mrs. Fisher looked from one to the other, then at me.

"Mr. Smith hit Gordy," I said. "I saw him do it. There was blood on the snow."

"Shut up, Magpie," Gordy said. "You too, Lizard."

Our voices brought Barbara to the top of the steps. Holding Brent, she smiled down at us. "Stu's awake now," she said. "Would you like to see him?"

Gordy was halfway up the steps before she finished speaking. Elizabeth and I were right behind him, but Barbara laid a hand on my shoulder, stopping both of us.

"Whoa," she said softly. "Let Gordy have a few minutes alone with his brother."

Elizabeth and I watched Gordy walk down the hall. His head was lowered, and he'd lost his swagger. From the back he didn't look very threatening. Seeing him hesitate outside Stuart's door, I realized I wasn't afraid of him anymore.

21

*A*fter Gordy disappeared, Elizabeth and I followed Barbara into her room. The first thing I noticed was a picture of Butch hanging on the wall over her bed. Tall and handsome, he smiled from the frame. He was wearing his high school football uniform and holding his helmet under his arm. Even though the picture was black and white, you could tell the sun was shining from the way he squinted into the camera.

A Hyattsdale High School pennant was tacked to the flowered wallpaper above Butch's picture, and a megaphone from Barbara's cheerleading days sat on the bureau next to another photo. In this one, Butch wore his army uniform, and Barbara stood beside him, a beautiful bride in a long white gown. They were brave to get married in the middle of a war, I thought, and it made me feel sad to look at their smiling faces.

Elizabeth flopped down on the floor to play with Brent, but I looked around the room, taking in everything it told me about Barbara. In her bookcase I saw six or seven Nancy Drews and a set of Winnie-the-Pooh stories mixed in with the kind of novels my mother read, *Gone with the Wind*, *A Tree Grows in Brooklyn*, and *The Robe*. Jammed in wherever they would fit were nursery rhymes, ABC books, and fairy tales.

A big teddy bear lay on Barbara's pillow, and a collection of Storybook Dolls stared down at us from a shelf over the window. On the radiator cover was an arrangement of china shepherds and shepherdesses, delicate ballerinas, and a couple of graceful horses.

Among all of Barbara's things, it was odd to see a baby's crib in one corner and a changing table in another. As further evidence of Brent's presence, a pair of Doctor Denton sleepers hung over the back of a rocking chair, and a set of alphabet blocks littered the floor.

While I stood in the doorway, Brent took a few cautious steps to Elizabeth. Squealing with delight, he threw himself in her arms and Elizabeth hugged him.

"When did he start walking?" Elizabeth asked.

"Last week," Barbara said proudly. "He won't be a year old till February second. Isn't he the world's smartest baby?"

While Elizabeth led Brent around the room by one hand, I sat down on the bed beside Barbara. "What did your folks say when they saw Stuart?" I asked her.

"Well, they were a little surprised," she said.

"They weren't mad?"

Barbara shook her head. "Dad was kind of upset that Stuart's family wasn't taking care of him," she admitted. "I told him Stu had an awful fight with his father, but I was worried he was going to walk over to Davis Road and give Mr. Smith a piece of his mind."

"How about your mother?" Elizabeth asked. "What did she say?"

"Oh, Mother's liked Stuart ever since the days in grade school when I dragged him home with me for milk and cookies," Barbara said. "The minute she saw him, she fixed up the guest room and put him to bed."

"I hope they don't find out he's a deserter," Elizabeth said.

Barbara picked up one of Brent's toys, a little rubber duck that squeaked when you squeezed it. Turning it round and round in her fingers, Barbara said, "I hate deceiving them, but I don't know what else to do. I'm scared to tell them the truth."

"Would your father turn him in?" Elizabeth asked.

"I don't think so," Barbara said. Giving the duck a couple of squeezes, she handed it to Brent.

He laughed and started chewing on the poor duck's head. Running her hand lightly over Brent's hair, Barbara smiled at him. Suddenly she leaned down and scooped him up in her arms. Giving him a fierce hug, she cuddled him on her lap.

"How can mothers let their sons go to war?" she asked Elizabeth and me. "If there's a war when Brent grows up, I'll tell him to hide somewhere like Stu."

"But Butch went," Elizabeth said. We all looked at his picture hanging over the bed. "He was a hero."

Barbara frowned. "I wish he'd stayed in his foxhole and let someone else throw that grenade. Then maybe he'd still be alive, maybe he'd be coming home to Brent and me when the war's over."

"But aren't you proud of his medals?" Elizabeth asked.

Without answering, Barbara walked to her bureau and opened the top drawer. Lifting something out, she laid it in Elizabeth's lap. It was a neatly folded American flag. On top of it lay two medals.

Elizabeth touched one as if it were a holy relic. It was a cross on a red, white, and blue ribbon. In its center was an eagle with upraised wings. "The Distinguished Service

Cross," she whispered. "Only the Congressional Medal of Honor is higher than this."

"He got it for exceptional heroism in combat," Barbara said. "That's what they told me when they gave it to me. He killed a nest of German machine gunners and saved a lot of other men's lives. But not his own."

Elizabeth's finger moved to a heart-shaped medal on a purple-and-white ribbon. In its center was George Washington's profile. "And this is the Purple Heart," she said. "You get this even if you're just wounded."

Taking the flag from Elizabeth, Barbara hugged it to her chest. "Of course I'm proud of Butch's medals," she said softly. "I just wish he hadn't had to die to get them."

Putting the flag back, she pushed the drawer shut and looked at us. "I don't really know what to think," she said, brushing her tears away. "I know how important this war is, but I hate it. The killing, the bombing, all the people who have to die because of Hitler and Mussolini and Hirohito. Why can't someone stop men like that before they start wars? That's what I want to know!"

Except for Brent's laughter as Barbara squeaked the duck, the room was so quiet I could hear the steam hissing in the radiator. I wished someone could answer Barbara's question. I would have liked to hear what they'd say.

*

After a while, Gordy came to the door. "My brother wants to see you dumbos," he said gruffly. Shoving his hands in his pockets, he walked back to Stuart's room, and we followed him.

When I saw Stuart, my heart turned over with relief. He

still looked sick, but he was propped up on clean white pillows. A blue satin quilt lay over him like a piece of summer sky, and, even though he was pale, his eyes were clear.

When he saw us, he smiled. "Well, well," he said. "Here are the angels of the battlefield again."

"You look better," Elizabeth said, rushing forward while I hung back, suddenly shy.

"Mrs. Fisher is a great nurse," Stuart said. "Not that you-all weren't," he added, "but she has better equipment." He pointed at the vaporizer puffing steam into the room and at the glass of ginger ale on a table by the bed. He had a big handkerchief tied round his neck like a cowboy's bandana, a treatment I recognized. Under it, his chest was no doubt slathered with Vick's Vapo-rub. I could smell it from the doorway.

"Come on in, Margaret," Stuart said, "and close the door. You're letting out the steam."

"Dummy," Gordy muttered at me as I hastily shut the door.

In a few minutes, the door opened again and Mrs. Fisher smiled at us. "Visiting time is over," she said. "Stuart needs lots of rest." She had a bottle of medicine in one hand and a spoon in the other.

Nicely as she spoke, we knew she meant it. We all left without protest, even Gordy.

*

Outside, our shadows were long and dark blue against the snow. The western sky was a lake of fire, and the trees looked like black lace against it. The wind had dropped, but it was still cold, and our breath made little clouds when we talked.

"Aren't you glad now that Barbara took Stuart to her house?" Elizabeth asked Gordy.

Angrily, he kicked at the frozen clumps of snow left by the plow along the roadside. He was wearing an enormous pair of rubber galoshes, which he hadn't bothered to buckle. Clink, clink, clink, they went as he stamped along.

"Her mother's a goody-goody," Gordy said. "And her father's a dope."

Elizabeth stopped right in front of Gordy. With her hands on her hips she glared at him. "How can you say that?" she yelled. "You must be the most ungrateful boy in the whole wide world!"

Gordy frowned at Elizabeth. In the light from the sunset, his face was rosy, but his eye looked even worse. "Just mind your own business and leave me alone, Lizard."

We watched him run off down the trolley tracks toward Davis Road. Elizabeth shook her head. "Every time I think I'm starting to like Gordy a little better, he acts horrible, and I hate him all over again," she said.

She was right. You could feel sorry for Gordy, you could try to help him, but he was like a stray dog who snarled and bit you when you tried to feed him.

"How come Stuart's so nice and Gordy's so awful?" Elizabeth asked as we walked along the trolley tracks. Answering her own question, she said, "Maybe Stuart got left on the Smiths' doorstep when he was a baby. It's hard to believe he's related to any of them."

*

When I got home, the first thing I noticed was the difference between our house and Barbara's house. No wreath hung on our front door, no Christmas tree stood in our living room, no Bing Crosby crooned "White Christmas" on our Victrola.

Later we might get a wreath and put up a tree, but my father hated Bing Crosby. Once I heard him ask Mother how she could swoon over a man whose ears stuck out. "He looks like a jackass and sounds like a sick cow," Daddy said. "He doesn't croon, he moos." Then he'd sing "White Christmas" in what he imagined was a cow's voice.

I liked Bing Crosby myself, and I thought Daddy could learn a lot from him. Not the way he sang—Daddy couldn't carry a tune, even he admitted that—but the way he acted. In all his movies, Bing was so kind and gentle and funny. He always understood how children felt; they could tell him anything and he would listen and give them good advice. If Daddy were like Bing Crosby, I could tell him about Gordy's father and he would know what to do.

At the dinner table, I asked Mother if we were going to get a tree. "Christmas is next Monday," I said. "That's less than a week away."

Before she answered, Daddy said, "What's the sense of celebrating? Your brother's not here, it's just us, and there's a war on."

"Jimmy wasn't here last year, either," I reminded him, "but we had a tree."

"And we'll have one this year," Mother said.

Daddy glanced at her as if he were going to argue, saw the frown on her face, and just shrugged. "Have one, then," he said.

"But you're the one who always chops it down," I said. "Mother and I can't go down in the woods and get it."

"Sure we can." Mother glared at Daddy, but he'd already left the table.

Sitting down by the radio, he tuned in "The Lone Ranger." At the sound of galloping hoofbeats, I followed Mother out to the kitchen.

"Don't you want to listen to 'The Lone Ranger'?" she asked.

"Not with Daddy." I leaned against Mother, and she put her arm around me. She didn't hug me very often.

"I know it's hard for you to understand, Margaret," she said, "but he's so worried about Jimmy he can't think of anything else. Christmas just isn't very important to him this year."

"Don't you think I'm worried about Jimmy, too?" I looked up at Mother, blinking hard to keep from crying.

"Of course you are." She pulled me closer and kissed my forehead. "But your father sees you outside with Elizabeth, laughing and playing, and he thinks you don't have a care in the world."

"Well, he's wrong," I told her. "I have more cares than he can ever know about."

"Oh, honey, don't be silly." Mother gave me a pat on the fanny, her way of dismissing my problems. Turning her back, she began running water in the sink. "Help me with the dishes like a good girl," she said.

22

*S*everal days later, Mother kept her promise about the Christmas tree. While Daddy was at work, she bundled herself up, grabbed a saw out of his toolbox, and walked down to the woods with me.

Daddy took pride in never having bought a tree. Before the war, he'd always taken Jimmy and me on an expedition to find our own. "A nice fresh one," he always said, "one we cut down ourselves. We don't want some old thing that's been lying around on a lot for weeks."

Last year he and I had gone, but now it was Mother and I who picked our way through the slushy snow and puddles, dragging the empty bobsled behind us.

Mother paused at the rusty fence and stared at the No Trespassing sign.

"The people who own the woods don't care if we cut down a tree," I said, quoting Daddy. "They'll never miss it."

"Your father told you that?"

I nodded. Somehow when Daddy said it, he made it seem perfectly natural to chop down a tree on somebody else's property. Standing here with Mother, though, I felt a little nervous. It was almost as bad as the first time I'd followed Elizabeth over the fence.

"Well, I hope your father's right." Mother looked around uncertainly as if she expected to see an armed guard protecting the trees, but all we saw was a crow perched on a limb, watching us.

Jerking on the rope, Mother managed to get the sled over the fence. As we entered the woods, I was glad Stuart was gone. Even if Mother saw the hut, she'd think a tramp had lived there for a while and then abandoned it when winter came.

Just to be safe, though, I steered her away from the hut toward a grove of pine trees on the other side of the woods. Most of them were skinny and crooked, but we finally found one Mother thought might do.

"We can tie branches on here and there to fill in the bare spots," she said.

Kneeling in the wet snow, Mother set to work with the saw while I held the tree steady. Even though it was much warmer than it had been earlier in the week, the wind still had a cold edge, and the sun kept sliding in and out of clouds. The snow had melted from the streets and sidewalks in College Hill, but in the woods it was still deep. Soon my toes and fingers were tingling, and I was glad when the tree finally sagged to the ground.

I helped Mother hoist it onto the sled. Slightly out of breath, she straightened up and smiled at me. Her cheeks were red, and her hair flew free around her face, making her look much younger. Tipping her head back, she laughed at the blue sky.

"Well, we did it without Walt," she said. "I knew we could."

Grabbing the rope, she eased the sled forward while I

made sure the tree didn't slip off. Busy with my responsibility, I didn't notice which path we were taking until we stepped into the clearing and came face to face with Gordy.

Although Elizabeth and I had visited Stuart several times, we hadn't seen Gordy since the day he'd run off down the trolley tracks. Now I stared at him, shocked. His eye was still bad, and his face was bruised in a couple of other places. He looked thinner, too, but he stood his ground and glared at me.

"Why, Gordy," Mother said. "What are you doing down here all by yourself?"

"Nothing, just taking a walk." Gordy shot me a look that clearly said I should drop dead on the spot, but Mother didn't notice. She was staring at his face.

"What happened?" Mother asked. "Have you been fighting?"

Gordy ducked his head, and his hair fell down, hiding some of the damage. "Me and some other guys were fooling around," he muttered.

"Well, come on, walk back with us." Mother looked at the hut and shivered. "There's no telling who hangs around a place like this."

"I'm okay," Gordy said. "I can take care of myself."

"What in the world?" Mother stared past Gordy. June was standing in the hut's doorway crying. Her face was bruised, too, and she was clutching Mittens the cat.

"I told you to stay in there!" Gordy yelled at June, but she just cried harder. Giving a frantic twist, the cat leapt out of June's arms and ran off into the trees. Mittens's escape made June cry harder.

Mother looked at Gordy. "What's going on?" she asked.

Ignoring Gordy, June ran through the snow toward Mother and me. All she had on her feet were slippers without socks, and her bare legs were mottled blue with cold. Her coat hung open, pinned at the neck. Under it she wore a skimpy gingham dress. Her hair was matted with tangles.

"Don't tell Daddy where we are," she begged Mother. "We have to hide so he won't beat us no more."

Mother picked June up. "Take the rope, Margaret," she said, pushing the sled toward me with her toe. "Gordy, you come with me right now."

"Where are you taking my sister?" He thrust himself in front of Mother, trying to block her path.

"Home," she said. "June can't stay here, and neither can you."

"To our house?" I asked Mother, running to catch up.

"To *their* house. I'm going to talk to Mrs. Smith."

"No," Gordy said. "No, you can't."

"I certainly can," Mother said. "Things like this have to be dealt with."

Ignoring Gordy's protests, Mother strode through the woods. Hurrying along behind her, I could see June's skinny little legs hanging down on either side of Mother's hips. One slipper fell off her foot, and Gordy picked it up.

"What about the tree?" I asked Mother when we reached the train tracks.

Mother turned around and stared at me as if she'd forgotten I existed. "For heaven's sake, Margaret," she said. "This is no time to be worrying about a Christmas tree. Just leave it. We'll get it later."

As I skidded down the slippery bank, Gordy grabbed my arm. "Do something," he whispered. "Make your mother stop sticking her nose in our business."

"If you think I can make my mother do anything, you must be nuts," I told Gordy.

"Well, she's going to be real sorry," Gordy said, "when she meets up with my old man."

"What will he do?" I stared at Gordy. Out of the corner of my eye, I could see Mother scrambling up the bank on the other side of the tracks. Her old green coat flapped in the wind as she reached the top.

"He'll cuss her out, for one thing," Gordy said. "Then who knows? Maybe he'll give both of you black eyes like mine."

My stomach tightened like a clenched fist, but I ran across the tracks and climbed up the bank. Mother was halfway down the block, striding through the puddles in her big rubber boots. June was watching us over Mother's shoulder, her arms wound tightly around her neck.

"Why did he hit June?" I asked Gordy. "What did she do?"

"Nothing, just got in his way. Her and that cat." Gordy ran ahead and caught up with Mother.

"Mrs. Baker," he said, "please don't go to my house."

But Mother was already turning the corner and heading down Davis Road, straight toward the Smiths' house. The old black Ford was parked out front. From the expression on Gordy's face when he saw it, I knew his father must be home. My heart fell like a rock to the bottom of my stomach, but I wasn't about to abandon my mother. If she was going to get a black eye, so was I.

Paying no attention to Gordy's pleas, Mother strode up the sagging steps and rang the bell. I stood behind her, starting at June's pale face. Her eyes were closed tight, but tears slipped out and rolled down her cheeks. She was clinging to Mother the way a shipwrecked sailor might cling to a life preserver.

Gordy waited beside Mother. He was holding one of June's hands and scowling at the closed door. I wished Elizabeth were here to see him. She would've been impressed by the tough way he stood there waiting for his father.

Mother pressed the bell twice more, but no one came. There wasn't a sound from the house. She turned to Gordy. "Do you think anyone is home?" she asked.

Gordy shrugged. "She's there," he said. "She just don't want to see anyone."

Mother knocked then, as hard as she could. "Mrs. Smith," she called. "It's Lillian Baker. I've got June and Gordy with me."

I heard footsteps, and the door opened a crack. Mrs. Smith peered at us. She looked worse than the last time I'd seen her. Like Gordy, her face was bruised. "My husband's sleeping," she whispered.

"Come outside," Mother said. "I want to talk to you."

"Just a minute." The door closed, and Mother looked at Gordy.

"It can't go on," she told him. "He mustn't be allowed to do this."

Gordy just looked at Mother. His eyes were flat and dull, and I knew he was wondering what Mother thought she could do to change anything. I wondered, too, but I was sure she had a plan.

The door opened again, and Mrs. Smith stepped outside. She'd put on a sweater, and she was holding the baby I'd seen before. Unlike Brent, he didn't smile or crow at the sight of us. He clung to his mother and regarded me solemnly with sad eyes.

"You mustn't get the wrong idea," Mrs. Smith told Mother. "I'm clumsy, I fall a lot, and the children, well, you know how kids are, they play so rough. You can't get through this world without a few cuts and bruises, everybody knows that. But I thank you for bringing Junie home. Gordy just drags her off sometimes, he loves her so much."

Her words tumbled out of her mouth, falling over each other. She reached for June with one arm while she balanced the baby on her hip with the other. "Come on, honey," she said, "let's get you inside. Gordy took you out without near enough clothes on."

But June buried her face in Mother's shoulder and refused to look at Mrs. Smith. "No," she cried. "No. Daddy hurt me, he hurt me."

Mrs. Smith's face turned red, and she tried to laugh. "Now isn't that silly, you bad girl, talking about your daddy like that. Gordy, I swear, you must be filling this child's head with craziness."

Gordy bent his head and stared at his feet. His hands stuffed in his pockets, his shoulders hunched, he looked older than Stuart. He said nothing.

"You come inside, Junie." Mrs. Smith seized June's arm and tugged, but the little girl refused to let go of Mother.

"Mrs. Smith," Mother said. "You can get help. You don't have to live like this."

Mrs. Smith glared at Mother then. "There's nothing

wrong with the way I live. Just because some don't have as much money as others in this town doesn't mean we have anything to be ashamed of. Now you put my daughter down and get out of here. I don't need any do-gooders sticking their nose in my business."

"Don't you have relatives?" Mother asked. "A mother, a sister?"

"What's going on?" Mr. Smith strode down the hall toward us, his footsteps loud in the sudden silence. Reaching the doorway, he shoved his wife aside and stared at Mother. He hadn't shaved, and his clothes were dirty and wrinkled.

At the sight of him, June cried harder. Gordy took her from Mother and pressed her face against his chest. Stroking her hair, speaking softly, he tried to comfort her.

Mother took a step or two backward, and I cringed behind her. At any minute I expected Mr. Smith to punch someone, maybe Mother, maybe me, maybe Gordy or June.

"This is Mrs. Baker, honey," Mrs. Smith said. Her voice was high and shrill enough to hurt your ears. "She just dropped by to say hello."

As Mrs. Smith babbled on and on about our social call, Mr. Smith continued to stare at Mother. His eyes were rimmed with red, and his cheeks bristled with gray whiskers. Mother looked at him as if she'd been turned to stone.

"Get out of here," Mr. Smith mumbled. "Go on, we don't need nothing from you."

Mother backed away, stumbling on Mittens, who must have followed us home from the woods. Regaining her balance, she grabbed my hand and led me down the steps.

Without looking back, she dragged me up Davis Road as if I were five years old. When we were around the corner, out of sight of the Smiths' house, Mother stopped and leaned against a tree.

"Margaret," she whispered, "I knew something was wrong, but I never dreamed it was so bad. People right here in College Hill living like that. I shouldn't have gone there, I should've listened to Gordy. I've probably just made things worse. Oh, that poor woman, those poor children. How can they bear it?"

Under spreading clouds, Dartmoor Avenue stretched before us, puddled with icy gray water. A melting snowman drooped in a yard. A dog trotted past, sniffing at the curb. Never had the town looked so dreary.

"There must be something we can do," I said. Surely Mother wasn't going to give up this quickly. Just a few minutes ago she'd been striding through the woods like a crusader out to save the world, but now her body sagged and her face looked as gray as the snow.

"Are you going to tell Mr. Crawford to arrest Mr. Smith?" I stared at Mother. Now that she knew the truth about Gordy, I was sure she'd fix his life the way she always fixed everything.

Without speaking, Mother took my hand again and started toward home. I looked up at her, expecting her to tell me what she meant to do. But she stared straight ahead and walked faster and faster, till I had to run to keep up with her.

Hidden behind dense clouds, the sun was setting. Lights

shone out of windows. Here and there I saw Christmas trees glowing in dark windows. Our tree was lying on the bobsled on the other side of the tracks, but it didn't seem worth mentioning now. Clinging silently to Mother's mittened hand, I let her lead me home.

23

*T*hat night while Daddy was listening to the news, Mother and I lingered at the dining room table. The moment we'd gotten home from Gordy's house, Mother had started dinner. She'd kept so busy, I hadn't had a chance to talk to her about the Smiths. But now, thinking she'd had plenty of time to come up with a plan, I asked her what we should do.

Mother set down her cup and stared at the tea leaves as if she expected to find the answer there. "You can't help a person if they won't admit anything is wrong," she finally said.

"Can't Mr. Crawford just go over there and arrest Mr. Smith?"

Mother patted my hand. "I know it's hard to understand, Margaret," she said, "but Mrs. Smith is the only one who can ask Mr. Crawford to do that."

"She's too scared," I said.

"It's a very unfortunate situation," Mother said. "But honestly, Margaret, there's nothing you or I can do."

Mother stood up and began gathering our plates and silverware. "It's time to clean up," she said.

As far as Mother was concerned, that was that. If Mrs. Smith didn't call the police, no one would. I glanced at her several times, but even when she handed me a dripping plate to dry, Mother didn't look at me. Her profile was stern, uncompromising, her nose sharp, her mouth set in a firm line. There was to be no more discussion of our visit to the Smiths'. Gordy's life was as cracked as the old platter I was drying, and Mother had no glue to fix it with.

*

The next afternoon, Mother and I went back to the train tracks. Our tree was lying on the sled where we'd left it, all alone in the melting snow. It looked as if it had been cut down for nothing.

Silently, we dragged the tree home and put it up all by ourselves. Even with extra branches tied on to fill in the worst gaps, it was too tall and skinny to be pretty. The glass balls and icicles and colored lights helped, but every time I looked at it, I thought about Gordy and June and Mrs. Smith.

After we came home from church on Christmas, our family exchanged gifts. Mother gave me a Sonja Henie doll. Dressed in a white skating costume trimmed with real fur, she smiled with parted lips to show her tiny teeth. As I examined her ice skates, Mother said it was hard to admit I was getting too old for dolls.

"You don't have to play with her," she said. "She's just so pretty, I couldn't resist her."

I laid the doll carefully back in her box. Her eyes closed, and I smiled at Mother. "She's beautiful," I said, "and I love her."

Thinking of Barbara's Storybook Doll collection, I decided to put Sonja in a safe place on top of my bureau. Unlike my old dolls, who were losing their hair, missing their toes, fingers, and most of their clothes, she would stay just the way she was now, as perfect as the day she was made.

While Mother and Daddy watched, I opened my other presents: a new Nancy Drew mystery, a collection of Edgar Allan Poe's stories, and a dark green sweater set. On the practical side, Mother had also given me an assortment of pajamas, underwear, and socks.

Snuggling up against Mother, I gave her my gift, the same brand of cologne she asked for every year. As usual, she pretended to be surprised and gave me a big kiss.

Daddy held up his present, a pair of argyle socks and a handkerchief, as if he'd never expected to receive anything like them. Then he and Mother gathered all the wrapping paper and tossed it into the fireplace. As the bright paper curled up in flames, Mother put an arm around me and hugged me.

"If only Jimmy was here," she said. "Last summer I was so sure he'd be home for Christmas, but now, well, I just don't know what to think." Turning away from me, she looked up at Daddy.

He shook his head and frowned. Without saying anything, he walked to the living room window and stared past Jimmy's blue star at the remains of the snow. Except for dinner, Christmas was officially over till next year.

*

Around two, I went to Elizabeth's house. In a small package was my gift for her, a pack of Double Bubble Gum and a Hershey Bar. Because of the medicine we'd bought for Stuart, neither of us had enough money for big presents.

The Crawfords always picked their tree from the Boy Scouts' lot, so it was bigger and far more beautiful than ours. At its base was a Swiss village of little cardboard houses surrounding an oval mirror meant to be a frozen lake. On its surface was a group of tiny metal ice skaters. Other figures stood in the village streets. On the outskirts was a farm, complete with livestock and tiny fir trees.

Every Christmas Mrs. Crawford set up the village. It was always the same. Each house had its own special place, each ice skater had his own special place, each cow, horse, sheep, and pig had its own special place. Even the goose girl's flock followed her in the same order. Ducks first, then chickens, geese last of all.

A Lionel train ran around the village, passing through tunnels and over bridges. No one but Mr. Crawford touched its controls. My father found that very amusing. He claimed Mr. Crawford secretly wanted to be God just to keep the trains running on schedule, but I wished we had a set just like it. I loved watching the engine go round and round, blowing its whistle and puffing out real smoke from tiny capsules.

As I knelt down to look for each little figure, I thought how nice it would be if College Hill were a Christmas village. Jimmy and Joe would be home, trading jokes and laughing. So would Donald and Stuart. Even Butch and Harold would be safe in their houses, eating turkey with their families. Every missing soldier would be in his place on the streets of College Hill.

"Want to see what I got?" Elizabeth poked me in the ribs to get my attention. She always received more presents than I did, mainly because she had lots of aunts and uncles who sent packages every year.

"Isn't she pretty?" Elizabeth held up a beautiful bride doll. "Aunt Marge says this is how I'll look on my wedding day."

Giggling at the thought of getting married, Elizabeth tossed the doll aside and rooted around in a pile of gifts to find the rest of her treasures—a pile of jigsaw puzzles and games, several Nancy Drews, a blue sweater set that matched her eyes, a variety of bubble bath sets, dusting powder, and three bottles of cologne. "Do you think someone's trying to tell me I have B.O.?" she asked.

At last she handed me my present and I gave her hers. Before opening them, we looked at each other. The packages were exactly the same size and shape. Laughing, we tore off the paper and discovered we'd given each other the same thing.

Popping a piece of the bubble gum in her mouth, Elizabeth jumped to her feet. "Let's go out for a while."

Lacy patches of snow lay mounded in shady places under bushes and trees, but the rest was gone. The sky was blue, and it was warm enough to leave our jackets unbuttoned. What both of us had really wanted—bicycles—we hadn't gotten. Daddy said you couldn't get one this year for love or money. So Elizabeth got on Joe's bike, and, with me behind her, she pedaled up Garfield Road, toward Beech Drive.

"We'll say 'Merry Christmas' to Stuart," Elizabeth said, steering the bike around puddles of melting slush.

The snowman in the Fishers' yard had shrunk to a couple of mounds about the size of softballs. Leaving the bike in the driveway, we rang the doorbell and Mrs. Fisher let us in.

"Just go on upstairs," she said. "Stuart's wide awake

and feeling much better. He should be on his feet next week."

Stuart grinned at us from bed. He and Barbara were playing a game of chess, and Brent was pushing a new wooden train around the floor, making little choo-choo sounds. The Victrola was playing "Swinging on a Star," and Stuart asked us if we'd ever carried moonbeams home in a jar.

We were all laughing when Gordy suddenly appeared in the doorway. He scowled as usual at the sight of Elizabeth and me, but Stuart beckoned to him.

"Come here, Gordo," he said. His voice was still hoarse, but he wasn't coughing as much.

"Merry Christmas," Stuart added as Gordy settled down beside him on the bed. His eye was better, and the bruises had faded. If you weren't very observant, you probably wouldn't have noticed them.

"Where have you been?" Stuart asked. "I haven't seen you for days."

Gordy shrugged. "I had stuff to do."

Stuart looked at him closely. "How're Mom and the kids?"

"They're okay." Gordy fiddled with the wrapper from the piece of chocolate Stuart had given him. He folded it smaller and smaller, creasing it with his thumbnail.

"It's the old man, isn't it?" Stuart took Gordy's face between his hands and lifted it gently toward him. In the soft light, he stared at the faded bruises. "That's why you didn't come. He hit you."

Gordy pulled away and slid off the bed. In the sudden silence, Bing Crosby was singing that you can be better than you are if you just swing on a star.

"I'm okay," Gordy said. "He did this the day we took you to the doctor. You were too sick to notice it then."

Stuart closed his eyes and lay back against the pillow. His face was chalky white. Alarmed, Barbara bent over him but he shook his head. "Here I am, lying in the lap of luxury, and Mom and the kids have nobody to protect them. What kind of a person am I? Scared to go to war, scared to hold a gun, scared of my own father."

"Stu," Barbara said, "don't talk like that. There's nothing you can do."

Stuart lay back and closed his eyes. Across the room, Gordy kept his back to us. He didn't say anything either. The Victrola needle went click, click, click, but nobody moved to turn it off.

"Choo-choo," Brent said. He crawled across the floor and pushed his train against Gordy's shoe. "Toot-toot."

Barbara scooped him up and hugged him, but he squirmed to get down. Still holding him, Barbara said, "Hasn't anyone tried to help?"

Gordy wheeled around and glared at me. "Stupid Magpie's mother came to our house, poking her nose in. Fat lot of good that did. You should've stuck around, you and your mother, to see what happened after you left."

He stared at me for a second. "Busted Mom's arm, that's what he did," Gordy said in a low voice. "Then he took her to the hospital and told them she fell down the basement steps. Come back again sometime, Magpie, if you and your mother want some excitement. Maybe he'll punch you out, too."

Elizabeth, Barbara, and I huddled together. The chess board had tumbled to the floor when Gordy jumped off the bed, and all the pawns and kings and queens lay scattered on the rug. The vaporizer hissed, the Victrola needle continued to click against the record, and Brent managed to wiggle out of Barbara's arms. Toddling across the floor, he picked up his engine and gave it to Gordy.

Gordy stared at the toy as if he had no idea what it was for. Then he zipped up his jacket. "I better go," he muttered to Stuart. "I just wanted to say 'Merry Christmas.' What a laugh."

"Hold on." Stuart pushed himself up in bed and started coughing again. "Give me my clothes," he said to Barbara. "I'm going with him."

"You aren't going anywhere!" Barbara stared at him. "Listen to that cough. Do you want to kill yourself?"

"It's okay, Stuart." Gordy bent over the bed. "You know how the old man is. He busted her arm, and now he's sorry. He threw out a whole bottle of whiskey, swore he'd never take another drink."

"How many times have we heard that?" Stuart asked. "He's probably going through the garbage right now, looking for it."

"No, he'll be okay for a while. He even brought home a tree and gave Mom some perfume." Gordy patted Stuart's shoulder. "Don't worry. I'm taking care of things."

Stuart frowned. "I can't keep hiding. Not from him, not from the war."

"Just stay here till you get well. Please?" Gordy lingered in the doorway, his eyes filled with worry.

"Are you sure everybody's all right?" Stuart stared at Gordy so hard you'd think he was trying to read his mind.

Gordy pointed to his face. "He hasn't touched me since the day Mrs. Goody-goody Baker tried to help."

Ashamed, I stooped down and started picking up the chess men. Mother hadn't meant to make things worse. Like me, she wanted to help.

After Gordy left, Barbara remembered the record. Lifting the arm, she turned the Victrola off and sat down beside Stuart. Brent climbed up on the bed and ran his train back and forth over the blue quilt.

"Well," Stuart said, looking from Barbara to Elizabeth and me, "it looks like Gordy and I aren't doing much to give you all a merry Christmas."

"It wasn't too merry, anyway," I whispered, thinking about Daddy standing at the window, staring at the blue star hanging there, worrying about my brother.

Nobody but Elizabeth heard me. On the way home, she said, "I know what you mean, Margaret. With Joe overseas, nothing's the same at our house, either."

"If only he and Jimmy would come home," I said. "Then everything would be all right."

Elizabeth glanced over her shoulder at me. "Sometimes I think the war will last forever," she said. "Nothing will ever be like it used to be."

Then she bent over the handlebars and pedaled hard. Picking up speed, the old Schwinn flew down the street, bouncing over ruts and splashing our legs and feet with icy gray slush.

24

*C*hristmas vacation dragged past, full of rain and wind and nothing to do but help Mother. After a week of vacuuming and dusting and polishing silver, it was a relief to go back to school. As much as I hated decimals and percentages, I hated housework more.

After what we'd been through together, I thought Gordy would be friendlier to Elizabeth and me, but he was just as nasty as ever. When I tried to catch his eye on the playground, he turned his head to the side and spit in the dirt. Even worse, he stole Elizabeth's lunch bag and ate everything except her apple. Looking her in the eye like he was daring her to tell, he threw the apple in the trash.

Elizabeth and I weren't the only ones Gordy was mean to. Except for Doug and Toad, he seemed to be mad at the entire world. Even Mrs. Wagner had trouble making him behave. As a result of talking in class, acting rude, and not doing his homework, Gordy spent a lot of time standing in the hall or staying after school scrubbing blackboards and pounding the chalk dust out of erasers.

No matter how Gordy felt, he couldn't keep Elizabeth and me from visiting his brother. Stuart was out of bed by the middle of January, but he was still too weak to do any more than sit in a chair. He looked better, though, and I thought he was beginning to gain a little weight.

One afternoon, Elizabeth and I were walking home

from the Fishers' house. Barbara was with us, pushing Brent in his stroller. He was too big for his carriage now, and he liked feeling the wind in his face. Opening his mouth, he gulped in air the way a dog does when it sticks its head out a car window.

"What's Stuart going to do when he gets well?" Elizabeth asked Barbara.

For a moment, Barbara didn't answer. We'd just crossed the trolley tracks, and she paused on the corner to wait for a car to go by. Dartmoor Avenue stretched ahead of us, long and straight, striped with the shadows of trees. A handful of leftover leaves whirled around our feet, and Brent leaned over the side of the stroller to see what was making the rustling sound under the wheels. He laughed and bounced up and down.

"I don't know," Barbara said. "Stu hasn't decided yet."

"Sometimes I think he should go back to the army," Elizabeth said, "and other times I think he shouldn't."

"He believes killing is wrong," Barbara said. "How can he go overseas feeling like that? It's not like the army needs Stu personally to win the war. Why can't they just leave him alone?"

Elizabeth glanced at her, but Barbara was bending over the stroller, checking on Brent. The wind had whipped red splotches on her cheeks, and her hair billowed around her face.

"Things are getting better in France and Belgium." Barbara straightened up and smiled at Elizabeth. "By the time Stu gets well, maybe it'll be all over, and he won't have to go anywhere."

Elizabeth nodded her head in agreement. "My father says the Russian army is beating the pants off the Nazis."

"We just got a letter from Jimmy yesterday," I added. "He says it's cold, and he's always hungry. He drew a funny picture of himself with a big fat stomach and under it he wrote, 'Me when I get home and eat Mom's cooking.'"

I looked at Barbara, but she was staring down Dartmoor Avenue at the brick houses sitting on their tidy squares of lawn, one little box after another. Her knuckles whitened as she gripped the handle of Brent's stroller. "Sometimes I can't believe there really is a war," she said slowly. "The whole thing seems like a story—until someone you love dies. Then you know it's real."

We walked on a little slower. I was thinking so hard I didn't see Gordy, Toad, and Doug until their bikes skidded to a stop in front of us.

"Oh, no," Elizabeth said. "Who let you out of the zoo?"

Ignoring Elizabeth, Gordy leaned toward Barbara. "How's Stuart today?" he asked. Instead of looking at her, he bent over to check his front tire. With his head down, the tips of his ears looked bright red.

"He's pretty good," Barbara said. "How about you?"

"Me? I'm fine."

"And your mother?"

Gordy glanced at Barbara. "She's fine, too, and so's my old man. He got a job at the defense plant across the tracks." The familiar nasty edge in his voice cut at my nerves, but Barbara didn't seem to notice.

"I'm glad to hear that," she said. "When are you coming to see Stu? He misses you."

Gordy shrugged elaborately. "With you around, I didn't think he noticed whether I was there or not." Turning to Toad and Doug, he said, "Come on, let's go."

We watched them pedal away, and Barbara sighed. A

gust of wind tossed her hair, and she brushed a long strand out of her eyes. Brent bounced in the stroller, and Barbara looked down at him as if she'd forgotten he was there.

"It's time for Brent's supper," she said. "I'll see you girls later."

The two of us watched her walk away. Before Barbara disappeared around the corner, she started running, pushing Brent faster and faster, making him laugh.

Elizabeth and I waved, hoping she'd look back and see us, but she kept on going. Silently, we turned toward home. The wind rattled the branches over our heads and sent cold fingers down the back of my neck. Except for Elizabeth and me, the street was empty.

Suddenly, Elizabeth gave a whoop and ran ahead. "Step on a crack," she shouted, stamping hard on the cement. "Break Hitler's back!"

"Step on a crack," I echoed, yelling as loud as I could. "Break Hitler's back!"

By the time we reached the corner of Garfield and Dartmoor, we were out of breath. As we leaned against Mr. Zimmerman's fence, trying to breathe normally, Elizabeth turned to me. The wind whipped her curls around her face, and her eyes sparkled. "I bet Barbara's in love with Stuart," she said. "That's why she doesn't want him to go to war."

"You're crazy," I said. "How could Barbara be in love? She has a baby."

Elizabeth rolled her eyes upward. "What on earth does Brent have to do with it?"

"Well, she's a mother, and mothers don't fall in love."

"Oh, Margaret, don't be such a dumbo." Giving me a

friendly shove, Elizabeth ran off down the street. A whirl-wind of leaves followed her, and she kicked them away.

"Last one home's a rotten tomato," she called to me as I sprinted along behind her. "See you tomorrow, Magpie!"

"Not if I see you first, Lizard!" I waved and hurried up my steps, pausing on the porch to return the face she was making at me. Then she ducked inside, the winner as usual.

Laughing, I shoved open the front door. As soon as I shut it behind me, I knew something was wrong. Daddy and Mother were sitting on the couch. Daddy had one arm around Mother. In his other hand was a telegram. They were both crying.

Motionless, I leaned against the door. My bones turned to water, and I couldn't speak, couldn't ask what was wrong. A huge, icy lump filled my throat, cutting off my breath. If I'd been able to move, I would have run out of the house. I didn't want to hear what they were going to say. Everybody knew what a telegram meant.

"It's Jimmy," Mother said at last.

I stared at her, paralyzed. The clock on the mantel chimed four-thirty, and a branch of the holly tree tapped against a window. On one side of the clock, Jimmy's face smiled at me from a silver frame, young and handsome in his uniform.

"He's been killed in action," Mother went on in a flat voice.

Crumpling the telegram into a tiny wad, Daddy hurled it into the fireplace. We watched it uncurl slowly on the cold hearth.

"But we just got a letter," I whispered. "There must be a mistake."

Not Jimmy, I prayed. Oh, please God, not Jimmy, not my only brother.

Mother hid her face in her hands. Her shoulders shook with sobs. Daddy touched her arm. Without saying anything, he left the room. In a couple of seconds the back door opened, then slammed shut behind him.

Mother and I stared at each other. Then she held out her arms, and I ran into them like a little child. Neither of us spoke. We just clung to each other and cried.

*

No one ate dinner that night. When Daddy came home several hours later, he told Mother he'd gone for a walk, but he smelled like beer and cigarette smoke. Silently, I watched him stumble into the bedroom and shut the door. In a few minutes, I heard him snoring.

Glancing at the kitchen clock, Mother said, "It's past nine. Go to bed, Margaret. There's nothing we can do now."

Holding me so tightly I couldn't breathe, Mother kissed me and sent me upstairs. I paused on the landing to look back at her. She was standing in the hall, one hand pressed against her mouth, tears sliding silently down her cheeks. I wanted to run back to her, to cling to her, to beg her not to send me away all alone, but instead I turned around and crept up the steps.

Before I went into my room, I tiptoed to Jimmy's door. Opening it slowly and quietly, I slipped inside and sat on his bed in the dark. Over my head, his model planes turned slowly in a draft creeping under the window. His miniature cars sat in a neat line on top of his bookcase. On the wallpaper, cowboys and Indians chased each other round and round the room. It was so quiet, I could hear my own breath going in and out, in and out.

"Let it be a mistake, God," I whispered. "Please don't let Jimmy be dead."

The wind shook the glass in the window and made a spooky sound in the eaves. A train whistle blew. A dog barked. Downstairs Daddy snored. I imagined Mother lying beside him, staring into the dark, still crying.

I went back to my own room and got into bed. "Don't be dead," I whispered. "Please, Jimmy, don't be dead."

*

The next day Elizabeth saw my face at my window and waved to me from her backyard. Grabbing my jacket, I went outside. Wordlessly, we walked down to the end of the yard and climbed up into the tree. Sitting on the platform Gordy had built for us, I shivered in the wind.

"Mother told me about Jimmy," Elizabeth whispered. "You must feel awful, Margaret."

I twisted a braid around my finger and then let it go, watching the coil of hair spring free. "It doesn't seem real," I said. "Jimmy's been over there for more than a year. When I woke up this morning, I couldn't believe it."

Elizabeth nodded. "Maybe the army made a mistake."

"That's what I've been hoping." I sighed and played with my braid, twisting it, untwisting it. "Sometimes it happens. There was an article in the *Star* not long ago about a soldier everybody thought was dead."

Elizabeth nodded. "I saw it. He was captured by the Germans, and they mixed him up with someone else."

Down the track, a train whistle blew. Elizabeth waved

to the engineer as the locomotive thundered past, but I didn't bother.

After it was gone, leaving nothing but smoke and cinders behind, Elizabeth said, "Do you feel any different about Stuart now? About his being a deserter and all?"

I thought for a moment and shook my head. "I wish Jimmy had deserted too. When he left, he told Mother not to cry. 'Nothing's going to happen to me,' he said. I can still hear him laughing at her for being so upset."

"Joe said the same thing," Elizabeth said. "I hope he was right."

"Maybe that's what soldiers have to believe. If they thought they were going to die, they wouldn't go."

We sat side by side, watching the clouds scud across the sky. The puddles in the alley had frozen again, and the wind tugged at us, but we stayed in the tree, ignoring the cold, as still as statues.

"Look, there's Gordy," Elizabeth said after a while.

Head down, hands jammed in his pockets, Gordy trudged slowly toward us. I didn't think he saw us, but when he was directly below us, he looked up. "I heard about Jimmy," he said. "I'm sorry, Magpie."

Then, while I stared at him, too surprised to say a word, Gordy walked on. Silently, Elizabeth and I watched him dwindle in the distance and finally disappear around a corner.

We looked at each other. Coming from Gordy's mouth, the words had a terrible, undeniable validity. Jimmy was dead. He wasn't ever coming home. Never, never in all my life would I see my brother again. While Elizabeth patted my back, I clung to the tree and cried.

25

The rest of January passed slowly, a series of cold, gray days. Even though we were pushing the Nazis back a little bit every day, I wasn't as excited as I once would have been. In some ways, it didn't make any difference to me what happened in Europe. Jimmy was dead. Nothing was going to change that. Not even victory and the end of the war.

Outside, icicles dripped from the eaves, puddles of gray slush froze, melted, and refroze, and birds sang sad winter songs from bare trees. Shivering in the wind, I walked to school with Elizabeth and tried to work hard for Mrs. Wagner. Sometimes I visited Stuart at Barbara's house, but often I made up an excuse to go home, and Elizabeth went without me. Although I was glad Stuart was getting better, it hurt me to see him. If Jimmy had stayed here in College Hill, he'd be alive too.

In my room, with just the radio to keep me company, I read and did my math problems while Mother fixed dinner. When Daddy came home, we ate silently. No one laughed, no one smiled. It was like we were walking underwater, pushing our way along the bottom of a murky lake, feeling our way toward something new. The sadness was so vast and heavy it filled up all the space in our house, suffocating everyone.

Mother spent a lot of time looking out the window. A few days after the telegram came, she bought a gold star at the dime store. Now it hung where the blue one used to hang. Like Mrs. Bedford, Mother touched Jimmy's star sometimes, tracing its outline with her index finger. I wanted to ask her what she was thinking about, but the sad expression on her face kept me from speaking.

Every night I prayed hard for Joe Crawford and Donald, harder than before because now I knew they could die. It was possible. Before Jimmy was killed, I really hadn't believed he would be hurt. I thought he'd be in the war for a while, the war would finally end, he'd come home, and life would be normal again. Daddy would joke and laugh, Mother would cook big dinners, Jimmy would draw pictures and make up funny stories. We'd be happy. All four of us.

Lying alone now in the dark winter nights, I knew our family was changed forever. The war would end soon, everyone said so, but Jimmy wouldn't come home. All we'd ever have was a box of his belongings and the letter from his commanding officer telling us he died bravely in the Ardennes during an assault on enemy lines. His body was buried in an American cemetery in Belgium. The commanding officer was sorry for Jimmy's loss; he said his sense of humor and courage would be missed. Daddy swore when he read the letter and said the officer didn't know the half of it.

In the box was a little sketchbook full of drawings of animals dressed like soldiers. Cats shot at dogs, mice attacked cats; wolves and bears wearing Nazi uniforms faced foxes in American uniforms. Daddy let me keep the pictures, even though some of them were scary, and I added them to my scrapbook. Then I put it away, not sure I wanted to look at Jimmy's drawings or letters again for a long time. My brother's war was over.

*

One Monday in February, something happened to take my mind off Jimmy for a while. Gordy came to school with a black eye. He scowled at me across the classroom as if he were daring me to say anything about it, and I stared down at my desktop, too sad to look at him. I didn't want to think about Mr. Smith cursing Gordy, hitting him, hurting him.

To avoid Gordy, I turned my attention to Mrs. Wagner. She was standing in front of a map of the world, using a yardstick to point out Iwo Jima. The marines had landed, she told us, and the Japanese army was fighting fiercely to drive them off the island. Slowly she moved the yardstick to Europe and showed us where the Russian army was fighting the Nazis in Poland. Then she moved on to the western front, where the Allies were slowly but surely pushing the Nazis back across the Rhine and into Germany.

As Mrs. Wagner described bombing raids and tanks and guns, I stole a glance at Gordy. He was bent over his desktop, carving a fighter plane into the wooden surface. While I watched he drew bombs dropping, one by one, with his pen. His lips moved, and I knew he was making silent explosions.

At recess, Elizabeth and I huddled against the wall of the school, out of the way of the kids playing dodgeball and jump rope. Across the playground Gordy, Toad, and Doug were sitting on the top of the monkey bars, pretending to be gunners. From where we stood, we could hear the "ackety, ackety, ack" of their artillery fire.

"I hope Stuart doesn't see Gordy today," Elizabeth said. "One look at that eye and Stuart might go home and have it out with his father, like he wanted to on Christmas. He's not strong enough to do anything like that."

She shoved her hands deeper in her pockets and hunched her shoulders against the wind. Even with her hair blowing in her face, I knew she was staring at Gordy.

As soon as school was out, Elizabeth and I went to the Fishers' house. If Gordy showed up, we planned to stop him from going inside, but he didn't come that day or the next. On Wednesday, Stuart asked us where his brother was.

Without answering, Elizabeth and I looked at each other. A mistake. From the expression on our faces, Stuart guessed we were hiding something. He was sitting in a chair beside his bed, wearing one of Mr. Fisher's old sweaters and the pair of jeans I'd taken from Jimmy's bureau drawer. He was still thin and pale, and his eyes had dark shadows under them. I was sure he wasn't well, not yet.

"It's the old man." Stuart put down the book of poetry he'd been reading, and Barbara laid her hand on his arm. "He's beating Gordy again, isn't he?" Stuart asked.

"No," Elizabeth said. "That's not it."

"Then where is he?" Stuart looked at Elizabeth and me.

My face heated up, and I stared down at the floor, unable to meet his eyes. "I don't know," I mumbled.

"We haven't seen him," Elizabeth said. "But he's all right."

"No," Stuart said. "He's not all right." He stood up and looked out the window at the brown grass and bare trees and tangled shrubbery. The sky was gray, and even the prettiest houses looked ugly in the dull afternoon light. "It can't go on."

"You can't do anything, Stu," Barbara said.

Without looking at her, Stuart went to the closet and found the old jacket he'd worn in the woods.

"Stu," Barbara said. "you mustn't go over there." She was on her feet now, standing between Stuart and the door.

In the quiet room, the jacket's zipper made a loud sound as Stuart yanked it up. "I have to," he said. "Can't you understand?"

"Your father will turn you in." Barbara grabbed his arm, but he shrugged her hand away. "Besides, you're not well." She hurried down the hall after him.

"Stuart, where are you going?" Mrs. Fisher met him at the bottom of the steps.

"Home," he said. Opening the door, he stepped out into the wind.

Barbara, Elizabeth, and I grabbed our coats and ran after him. By the time he'd reached the trolley tracks, he was coughing.

"Stu, please," Barbara said, "be sensible."

Elizabeth and I plucked at his sleeve, but he ignored all three of us and kept walking.

"They'll send you to war," I screamed at him. "You'll die!"

But he didn't listen to any of us. At the corner of Davis Road, he paused and looked down the street. There in front of his house was the old black Ford.

Turning to Barbara, he said, "Go home. Please, Barb, let me handle this my way."

"What are you going to do?" she said.

"Talk to him, that's all. Make him see."

"See what?" The wind whipped Barbara's hair and ballooned her coat.

Stuart didn't answer. He walked down the street with the three of us at his heels. At his gate, he looked at Barbara. "Thanks for everything," he said. "No matter what happens, nobody will ever know you or your family were involved in any way."

Stuart paused and looked at each of us. "As far as you all know, I've been hiding in the woods since last summer."

Barbara began to cry. While Elizabeth and I watched, Stuart put his arm around her. Clinging to her for a moment, Stuart kissed her. Then he let her go and climbed the front steps slowly.

"Please leave now," he said to us before he opened the door and went inside.

Barbara stood at the gate, one hand gripping the latch, and stared at the house. Nothing happened. The window shades stayed down, the door stayed shut. While we watched, Mittens came out from under the porch, slunk up the steps, and sat down by the milk box.

Barbara looked at Elizabeth and me. "Let's go," she whispered. Brushing the tears from her eyes, she turned her back on the Smiths' house.

For a moment I thought Elizabeth would protest, but, without saying a word, she followed Barbara and me up the street. Her head down, the wind tugging at her curls, Elizabeth looked as defeated as my mother had the day we walked home from our visit to the Smiths' house.

On the corner, Barbara hesitated. Gordy was pedaling toward us on his bike, his face flushed from the wind. Slamming on the brakes, he skidded to a stop a few inches from us.

"What are you doing here?" he asked.

Barbara started to cry again, leaving it to Elizabeth to answer. "Stuart was worried because you hadn't been to see him," she said. "He guessed about your father hitting you, and he went to your house. He's there right now. We tried to stop him, but he went anyway."

Gordy's face turned white. I was standing so close to him I could see the constellations of freckles on his face, the tiny network of blue veins at his temples, the purple scar over his eyebrow, the yellowing bruises on his face. For a moment I wanted to reach out and touch the scar, but Gordy was already racing away from us.

Silently, we watched him swerve through his front gate, ditch the bike, and run up the front steps. The door slammed shut behind him with a bang loud enough to startle a pair of sparrows away from their perch on the telephone line.

"Now what?" Elizabeth looked at Barbara, but she was still crying.

Elizabeth turned to me. "What should we do?"

"I don't know." Looking at Barbara, I felt like crying, too. What I really wanted to do was go home. It was time for "Captain Midnight," and I wished with all my heart I could be a little kid again, sitting on the floor by the radio with my special decoder badge, waiting for the secret message. Jimmy would be sitting at the dining room table complaining about his homework, and Mother would be out in the kitchen singing "Chattanooga Choo Choo" while she fixed dinner. How could everything have changed so much in just four years?

While I stood there silently, Elizabeth patted Barbara's arm. "Don't cry," she said gruffly. "Stuart will be okay. Gordy will straighten it all out."

Like a child, Barbara wiped her eyes with the back of her mitten and sniffled. She'd never bothered to button her coat, and it flapped around her like bat wings in the wind.

"You girls go home," she whispered. "I'll see you later."

Without looking back, Barbara walked away slowly, leaving Elizabeth and me to trudge home through the winter dusk by ourselves. It was getting colder, and we hunched our shoulders against the wind.

"What do you think will happen to Stuart?" Elizabeth asked me.

"Mr. Smith will turn him in," I said. "Then the army will send him to war."

"That's what I think, too," Elizabeth said. "I hate Mr. Smith. Next to Hitler, he's the worst man in the world."

"They should send him to war instead of Stuart," I said.

Elizabeth nodded. "They should put him in the front line and let the Nazis kill him. That's what he deserves."

We were standing in front of Elizabeth's house. Even though it wasn't dark yet, the lights were on. They made her house look warm and cozy.

Halfheartedly, I stamped on the sidewalk. "Step on a crack," I said, "break Mr. Smith's back."

Elizabeth joined me, and our voices rang out like steel in the icy air. "Step on a crack, break Mr. Smith's back! Step on a crack, break Mr. Smith's back!"

While we were shouting and stamping Mr. Smith to a

pulp, Elizabeth's door opened, and Mrs. Crawford looked out at us. "Come inside, Elizabeth," she called. "You'll catch your death out there in the cold."

Turning away, I ran up the sidewalk to my house. A light shone from my living room window, too, silhouetting my brother's star. Backlit, it was black just like the star in the Crawfords' window. From here you couldn't tell that Jimmy's was gold and Joe's was blue.

26

When I opened the front door, I saw Mother sitting on the couch. On her lap was a folded flag, and on it were two medals. The room was very quiet. All my fears for Stuart flew right out of my heart. Clutching my schoolbooks to my chest, I stared at her, waiting for her to tell me what had happened.

"Some men from the army came today," Mother said. "They brought Jimmy's medals."

Still weak in the knees, I sank down beside her. Pointing to one of the medals, Mother said, "This is the Silver Star. He got it for gallantry in action. And this is the Purple Heart."

In the silence the clock on the mantel ticked. Neither of us spoke. We sat there side by side, staring at Jimmy's medals. For this little star on a red, white, and blue ribbon, for this heart my brother died. I remembered the afternoon Barbara showed me Butch's medals. Who decided which ones a soldier received? Was Butch braver than Jimmy because he got the Distinguished Service Cross instead of the Silver Star?

Biting my lip, I frowned at the medals, trying to find some consolation in them, in what they stood for, in the knowledge my brother died bravely. To me they were just pretty decorations. They were no substitute for Jimmy's living presence.

"They were very nice, the young men who brought them. Tall and handsome in their uniforms, like Jimmy was," Mother said. Her voice was low and hoarse, and I suspected she'd cried after the soldiers left. It made me even sadder to think of her all alone crying over the medals.

"They told me I should be proud of Jimmy," she went on. "He died for his country. He was brave. A hero."

Mother sighed, and a tear splashed down on the flag folded so neatly on her lap. Looking past me at the gold star in our window, she frowned. "How does God choose who dies and who lives?" she asked.

Without waiting for an answer, she got to her feet and laid the flag and the medals on the coffee table as gently as a mother might lay a baby in a crib. "Your father will be proud to see these," she said to me.

In a few moments, I heard her rattling pots and pans in the kitchen. Soon Daddy would be home, asking if dinner was ready.

I stood in the doorway and watched Mother pare three potatoes. There were so many questions I wanted to ask her, so many things I wanted to tell her, but she kept her back turned, busying herself with chores. Suppose I told her what Stuart had said about killing? Or what Barbara had said about Butch's medals? Like her, did Mother secretly wish someone else had won that Silver Star? Trying to get her attention, I cleared my throat, but Mother didn't look at me. Silently, I gathered up my schoolbooks and went upstairs to begin my homework.

With so many worries weighing me down, it was hard to keep my mind on my vocabulary exercises. Usually I loved learning new words and putting them into interesting sentences, but not this evening. Shoving my notebook and dictionary aside, I went to the window and pressed my face against the cold glass. The houses across the alley huddled behind a scraggly line of fences and hedges. Beyond them was a ball field, then a little woods, then Davis Road. Hidden by the roofs and trees, the Smiths' house was just a few blocks away. If only I knew what was happening there.

*

The next day, Gordy was absent from school. At recess Elizabeth and I asked Toad and Doug if they knew where he was. They looked at each other, and I knew they were worried.

"We waited for him on the corner," Doug said, "but he didn't come."

"So we went to his house," Toad put in. "We knew things were bad with his father and all."

"But it looked deserted," Doug went on. "The blinds were pulled down, and nobody came to the door. We walked around back, but we didn't see anybody."

"I saw a curtain move upstairs," Toad said.

Doug made a snorting noise. "You didn't see anything, you dope."

Toad scowled and kicked a stone across the playground. "Something's wrong in that house," he insisted. "I just know it."

Doug snorted again. "Don't pay any attention to Toad," he said to Elizabeth and me. "He listens to too many scary radio shows. He can't even sleep at night unless he's got the hall light shining in his room. He thinks the Shadow's coming up the steps to get him."

Doug leaned close to Toad and imitated the Shadow's

laugh. "Who knows what evil lurks in the hearts of men?" he hissed in Toad's ear.

Despite Doug's ridicule, I felt chills race up and down my neck. Toad's face was red, and he was arguing with Doug, denying he kept the hall light on, claiming "The Shadow" was a dumb show, calling Doug a liar.

"You mean you knocked and nobody came to the door?" Elizabeth asked, butting into their quarrel.

The boys nodded, agreeing now. "All we saw was a cat sitting on the porch," Doug said.

"Was the car out front?" Elizabeth wanted to know.

"That beat-up old Ford Mr. Smith drives?" Doug asked.

"Yeah," Toad said, "it was there. That's why I think something's wrong." He glared at Doug, daring him to argue the point again.

The recess bell rang, and we ran across the playground. Sliding into my seat, I opened my big blue geography book and tried to pay attention to Mrs. Wagner, but it was hard to think about the major resources of Idaho. I couldn't keep my eyes away from Gordy's empty desk. It sat there, three rows from mine, its top scarred with doodles of bombers and battleships, a silent reminder of him.

*

When school was out, Elizabeth and I ran all the way to the Fishers' house, but as soon as Barbara opened the door, we knew Stuart wasn't there. Her eyes were red and swollen, and her face was pale.

"I've gone over to the Smiths' two or three times today," Barbara said, "but nobody comes to the door. I'm sure someone's home. I could almost hear them listening to me knocking."

Elizabeth and I looked at each other. Toad was right, I

thought. Something was wrong. I knew it in the marrow of my bones.

And Elizabeth knew, too. Grabbing my hand, she dragged me out of the Fishers' house. Without saying a word, we ran across the trolley tracks and headed toward Davis Road. With the wind at our backs, we rounded the corner and then stopped, stunned by what we saw.

A police car and an ambulance were parked in front of the Smiths' house. While we watched, Elizabeth's father came down the front steps with Mr. Smith. From where we stood, Elizabeth and I could see the handcuffs binding Mr. Smith's wrists behind his back. He didn't look as big and fierce as he had the last time I'd seen him. His head was bent, his shoulders hunched, his walk unsteady. While a crowd of neighbors stared, Mr. Crawford shoved Mr. Smith roughly into the back seat of the police car and slammed the door.

Then two men carrying a stretcher made their way carefully out of the house. Gordy was right behind them. The back doors of the ambulance stood open, and the men pushed the stretcher inside. When Gordy tried to climb in after it, one of the men shook his head. The doors closed, the light flashed, and the siren started. Away went the ambulance. Right behind it was the police car.

Mrs. Smith stood on the front porch and watched the two vehicles speed past Elizabeth and me. When they turned the corner and disappeared down Dartmoor Avenue, she covered her face with her hands. June and the two little boys clung to her skirt. The baby toddled back and forth, chasing Mittens.

As the sound of the sirens faded away in the gray air, we ran down the street toward Gordy. His back was turned, but when he heard our footsteps, he wheeled around to confront us.

Elizabeth and I stopped and stared at him, speechless. His face was a mass of bruises, and tears were seeping out of his swollen eyes. I thought he would yell at us, curse us, chase us away, but he just stood there. The expression on his face reminded me of a photograph I'd seen in *Life* of a soldier suffering from battle fatigue. The weariness and sorrow in his eyes made me hurt inside.

There was a cry behind us, and I turned to see Barbara running toward us, her coat billowing around her. Wordlessly, she threw her arms around Gordy and drew him close. To my amazement, he clung to her like a child and wept.

"What happened?" she asked him. "Where's Stuart?"

"Dad beat him last night," Gordy sobbed. "He wouldn't fight back, Barbara, he just tried to keep the old man from hurting the rest of us. Mother was so scared she dragged us all in the bedroom and locked the door, she shoved a chest in front of it, too. The old man had a baseball bat, he tried to break down the door, and when he couldn't, he smashed up the house." Gordy started crying again. "All night he kept us up there. I thought Stuart was lying downstairs dead."

Elizabeth grasped my arm so tightly I could feel her fingernails bite right through the sleeve of my jacket. "How did you get out?" she asked Gordy.

"Mother wouldn't let us open the door. She said he'd kill us all. So we stayed in the room, but finally I opened the window and yelled for help. Mother didn't want me to, she didn't want anyone to know, she thought maybe he'd just sleep it off and everything would be okay.

But the lady next door heard me and called the cops."

"Where is Stuart?" Barbara asked again, louder this time. "What happened to him?"

"They took him to the hospital," Gordy whispered. "The old man almost killed him."

"Oh, my God," Barbara whispered. "Oh, my God."

Elizabeth and I stared at each other. My mouth was too dry to speak. My arms and legs felt weak, too. I saw Stuart in that soft white bed in the Fishers' house, cozy and safe under the blue quilt. After being so sick, he'd gotten well only to have his own father hurt him.

"He beat you, too, didn't he?" Elizabeth asked Gordy.

"No worse than other times." Gordy tried to wipe his tears away, but he winced with pain when he touched his face.

"There should be a deep, dark dungeon where people like your father could be chained to the wall forever and forever," Elizabeth said. "Him and Hitler and Mussolini and Hirohito. They should all be there."

"What's your mother going to do?" Barbara asked Gordy.

"Take us to our grandmother's house," he said, "down in North Carolina. She never wants to see the old man again, not after what he did to Stuart. This time she better mean it."

Gordy tried to toss his hair back and look tough, but he didn't quite succeed. "We'll get out of this town as soon as Stuart's better," he said, glancing at the neighbors standing in a little group, talking quietly. "It can't be soon enough for me." Gordy spat into the mud puddle at his feet and turned away.

"Wait!" Barbara seized his arm and drew him back. "Where did they take Stuart?"

"Some army hospital," he said. "They know he deserted."

This time Barbara let Gordy go. We stood on the sidewalk and watched him run up his front steps. Mrs. Smith had taken the younger children inside, but Mittens still crouched hopefully on the porch.

Gordy opened the door, but before he went inside he turned and looked back at us. "Thanks, Barbara," he said. "You too, Lizard, Magpie. You done your best. The way things worked out, it wasn't your fault."

He went into the house, and Mittens darted through the door behind him.

Barbara put an arm around Elizabeth and an arm around me. "Come on," she said, hugging us against her sides.

"Do you think Stuart will be all right?" I asked Barbara.

She squeezed my shoulders even tighter. "I hope so, Margaret. I'll find out where he is and go see him."

"Can we come with you?" Elizabeth asked.

I ducked my head, embarrassed. Sometimes Elizabeth just didn't have any sense.

Barbara gave Elizabeth a hug. "I'll let you know what I find out. Okay?" She tried to smile, but her eyes were still watery with tears.

At the corner, the three of us paused and looked back down Davis Road. On Dartmoor Avenue, lamps glowed in windows, warming the dusk, but the Smiths' house was as gray and cheerless as the cloudy sky. One crack of light shone out from under a drawn shade in the living room. Even from here, I could feel the unhappiness in the house.

27

*G*ordy wasn't in school the next day. If it hadn't been pouring down rain, Elizabeth and I would have gone to his house, but even our umbrellas and boots didn't keep us dry. We were soaked by the time we got home.

"Daddy says Mr. Smith won't be in jail long," Elizabeth told me. We were on her front porch, and the rain pouring off the eaves curtained us from the street. It was like being behind a waterfall.

"They charged him with being drunk and disorderly," Elizabeth went on, "but if Mrs. Smith doesn't accuse him of anything else, he'll be free as a bird in no time."

"It's not fair," I said. "The police should know she's scared of him. Wouldn't you be afraid to make him mad?"

For an answer, Elizabeth clenched her fist and pretended to sock Mr. Smith. "Not me," she boasted. "If I ever get married and my husband treats me bad, he'll be sorry."

In silence we watched the rain. It was coming down so hard that drops the size of silver dollars bounced up from the sidewalk. Garfield Road was a sheet of muddy brown water. A car passed slowly, up to its hubcaps in puddles. It left a wake behind like a boat.

While we stood there, I heard a door open. Looking at my house, I saw Mother on the porch, peering through the rain and frowning. "I wondered where you were, Margaret," she said. "Come on home before you catch your death. I bet you're soaked."

After I'd put on an old pair of Jimmy's overalls, I sat down at the kitchen table. Mother set a cup of steaming Ovaltine in front of me, and I drank it slowly, enjoying the taste of chocolate and the little trace of bitter iron it hid. Outside, drops of rain slid down the windowpane as if they were racing each other. You could hypnotize yourself watching them.

"Well." Mother's voice broke into my trance. "I suppose you know about the goings-on yesterday at the Smiths' house."

I stared at her solemnly over the rim of my cup. The clock ticked cheerfully, and the rain drummed against the glass, making the kitchen safe and warm. Mentally, I contrasted our house with the Smiths' house, where no one was safe, not even Mrs. Smith.

Leaning toward Mother, I said, "Elizabeth and I saw Mr. Crawford take Mr. Smith away in his police car, and then they took Stuart to the hospital in am ambulance. Do you know if Stuart's okay?"

"According to one of the neighbors, Mr. Smith beat Stuart unconscious. He fractured his skull and broke his arm." Mother looked down at the table and moved her finger along one of the patterns painted on its metal surface.

"Maybe I should have told Mr. Crawford about the day we went to that house with Gordy and June," Mother said, "but I just turned my back and tried to forget what I'd seen. All my life I've believed you shouldn't interfere in other people's business, but now I feel bad, especially about that poor woman."

"How about Stuart?" I asked her. "He's the one who's really hurt."

"Did you know he was hiding in that hut in the woods?" Mother asked. "Is that why you tried to steer me away from it the day we cut the tree down?"

With her looking me straight in the eye, I couldn't lie. Feeling important, I said, "We were helping Stuart, Elizabeth and me." Defying her to punish me, I added, "He was sick, and we brought him food and medicine. We probably saved his life."

For a moment Mother didn't say anything. She sat very still, staring at me as if I were a stranger. "You helped a deserter?" she said at last, her face pale. "You went down there in the woods where you are absolutely forbidden to go and helped a *deserter?* When you own brother was overseas fighting for his country?"

"Yes," I said, "that's just what I did. And I'm glad of it. Just because Stuart didn't want to go to war and kill people doesn't mean he's bad."

"He's a *coward*," Mother said, her voice full of ice. "And I'm ashamed of you!"

Tears sprang to my eyes. It wasn't till now that I realized I'd wanted Mother to be proud of me for helping Stuart. Hadn't she said she liked him, that he was her favorite paperboy? Now she was behaving as if he weren't even human.

Ignoring my tears, Mother said, "How do you think Jimmy would feel if he knew his own sister was helping a deserter while he lay dying in Belgium?"

"It wasn't like that!" I said, stung by the unfairness of her question. "Stuart was sick, he *needed* me! I wish Jimmy had been down there in the woods, too! Then he'd be alive, not dead!"

Mother slapped me then, as hard as she could, right in the face. "Never say anything like that again!" she cried. "Never! Your brother died for his country, he paid the price so we could live in a better world when this war is over! Go to your room! And stay there!"

"You don't understand anything!" I shouted at her, and then I ran up the stairs two at a time. Slamming my bedroom door, I threw myself down on the bed and wept. My heart was full of rage at the unfairness of everything. I hated Mother, I hated Hitler, I hated Mr. Smith.

I must have cried myself to sleep, because the next thing I knew my room was dark and I was still lying on my bed, shivering in the cold. The only sound was the rain pelting against the windows. Then I heard Mother's footsteps on the stairs. Closing my eyes, I rolled over and faced the wall. For once, Mother could look at my back and see how she liked being ignored.

"Margaret?" Mother opened my door, and a ray of light from the hall fell across my bed.

When I didn't say anything, she sat down beside me. Touching my shoulder, she leaned over me, trying to see my face.

"Margaret," she repeated, "I know you're not asleep. Please sit up. I want to talk to you."

Reluctantly, I did as she asked, but I kept my head turned away from her.

"I'm sorry I hit you," Mother began. "I lost my temper. I know that's no excuse, but I was so mad."

"Probably Mr. Smith tells Gordy the same thing after he beats him up," I muttered.

Mother swallowed hard and turned my face toward her, forcing me to look at her. "I'm still angry about your helping Stuart," she said. "Desertion is wrong, Margaret, and if anyone finds out what you did, you could get into a lot of trouble."

I shrugged. "Even if I go to jail, I'll still be glad I helped Stuart."

Mother sighed. "You're just a child, Margaret," she said. "If you were older, you'd understand how serious this war is."

I didn't argue, but in my heart I was sure Mother was wrong. My feelings didn't have anything to do with being a child except I couldn't put them into words. I knew the war was serious, I knew we had to stop Hitler, but if you truly believed killing was wrong, what were you supposed to do?

"Stuart ran off and hid in the woods," Mother went on. "Did that make the war end any sooner? Did it save any lives except his own?"

I twisted one of my braids around my finger so tightly it hurt, but I didn't have an answer. It was so confusing. All I could see was Stuart's sad face, pale and thin, almost hidden by his hair and beard, the way he'd looked when I first met him. I could hear him say, "Killing is wrong, I can't do it, I won't shoot anybody." I thought about the poem he'd asked Elizabeth and me to read to him, the one about the soldier who would've preferred to drink a beer with his enemy instead of shooting him.

"People like Stuart are different," I finally told Mother. "You can't judge him the way you judge other people.

Jimmy called him the little poet. He would've wanted me to help Stuart, I *know* he would have."

"Don't bring Jimmy into this," Mother said.

"Why not?" I stared at her. "Jimmy liked Stuart. He took up for him when the other boys teased him. He knew Stuart couldn't defend himself."

Mother sighed and ran a hand through her hair. In the dim light, her eyes sought the picture of Jimmy on my dresser. She stared at his smiling face as if it might tell her something, but my brother was as silent as my Sonja Henie doll poised on her skates beside the photograph.

After thinking for a while, Mother said, "Jimmy felt sorry for Stuart. Like you, he wanted me to do something about Mr. Smith, but I never did."

The rain gusted against the window, and a train blew its whistle down the tracks. Otherwise it was very quiet in my room.

"Stuart's had a hard life," Mother went on slowly, as if she were finding excuses against her will. "He wasn't rough and tough like his brothers. I still remember him as a little boy crying over a squirrel Donald shot with an air rifle."

"That's what I mean," I said. "Stuart can't stand to see anything hurt. Not a squirrel, not a person."

"Neither could Jimmy," Mother reminded me. "But he went to war, he did what he had to do even though it killed him."

I sighed. We'd gone in a circle, and now we were right back where we'd started from. There was no answer, no firm ground to stand on. Leaning against Mother, I felt her arm close round me, as if she wanted to protect me from the cracks I saw opening everywhere.

"Come down to dinner," Mother said softly. "Your father's waiting to eat."

"Did you tell him about me and Stuart?" I asked, suddenly fearful. It was one thing to make Mother mad. She'd get over it. But I wasn't sure about Daddy. He might never forgive me.

Mother shook her head. "I thought about it," she said, "but he'd be more upset than I am."

As we started downstairs, she turned and looked back at me. "One thing I've learned from this," she said, "is to pay more attention to you, Margaret. I had no idea what you and Elizabeth were up to. If I hadn't been so preoccupied, I might have noticed."

Silently, I followed her into the dining room and took my place at the table. Daddy was already seated, the *Evening Star* spread open beside him. "Look at this," he said, "we've taken two more bridgeheads over the Rhine." His finger stabbed at the headlines, and he smiled at Mother and me. "It won't be much longer now," he said.

*

The next day Mrs. Wagner told our class that Gordy wasn't coming back to school. "His family has moved to North Carolina," she said.

Elizabeth and I stared at each other, shocked. Gordy had left already? Without even saying good-bye? I looked at his empty desk. His books and papers were there, as untidy as ever. How could Gordy be gone?

As soon as the dismissal bell rang, Elizabeth and I went to the Smiths' house. The rain had stopped, but we were wearing boots to keep our shoes dry. We slopped through puddles in the road, making muddy waves with our feet. The damp sidewalk was littered with dead pink worms, but here and there a crocus poked up on someone's lawn. It was almost March, the sky was blue, washed clean even of clouds. Despite this, Davis Road still had a dreary winter look.

The first thing we noticed was the absence of the old Ford. That gave us the courage to push open the rusty gate and approach the house. The shades were drawn, the door was closed, no smoke rose from the chimney. I hung back, but Elizabeth ran lightly up the steps and knocked loudly. After several tries, she looked over her shoulder at me.

"Nobody's here," she said. Going to the window, she found a tear in the shade and peered inside.

Cautiously, I joined her. The house was dark, but gradually I made out the room's shape. It was empty except for trash. Old papers, broken toys, dirt and dust, a child's striped sock. Mrs. Wagner was right. The Smiths were gone.

We stared at each other, lost for words. A few months ago nothing would have made us happier. We would have been dancing in the streets to celebrate Gordy's departure.

"I always thought we'd see him again," Elizabeth said. "Didn't you?"

I nodded. Together we walked around the house, taking in the peeling paint, the sagging porch, the worn steps, the grassless yard. The broken swing twisted in the breeze. Of Mittens there was no sign. I hoped they'd taken the cat with them.

Silently, we opened the gate, taking care to latch it behind us, and trudged home through the puddles on Davis Road. Even now, even knowing he was gone, I expected to see Gordy pedaling toward us on his rusty old bike, his black hair flying back from his face, yelling threats or insults at Elizabeth and me. We'd been fighting Gordy for so long, I couldn't imagine a future without him. He'd come back, I told myself, surely he would.

28

*S*everal weeks later, Elizabeth and I were spending a Saturday afternoon in the Trolley Stoppe Shoppe, sitting at the counter and sipping cherry Cokes. A group of college students was feeding nickels to the jukebox, and we were listening to the music and watching them dance. At the moment, Elizabeth was twirling round and round on her stool in time to "Boogie Woogie Bugle Boy." Proud that she knew all the words, she was singing along with the Andrews Sisters and driving me crazy.

"Quit spinning," I said. "You're making me dizzy."

She laughed and spun so fast the guy behind the counter told her to stop before she fell off and hurt herself. Elizabeth gave him one of her sassiest looks, but before she could think of a good wisecrack, I nudged her.

"Look, there's Barbara," I said, pointing through the big plate-glass window. On the other side of the street, Barbara was pulling Brent along the sidewalk in his red wagon.

Launching herself from her stool, Elizabeth ran to the door, and I dashed after her. We hadn't seen Barbara since the day the ambulance took Stuart away.

When she saw us running toward her, Barbara smiled

and waved. "Well, long time no see," she said. "Where have you two been?"

"Mrs. Wagner keeps us busy with so much homework we haven't had time to do anything," Elizabeth said.

Neither one of us wanted to admit that our mothers had confined us to our own yards for the past three weeks as a punishment for helping Stuart. At first Elizabeth had been furious because my mother had told her mother what we'd done, but after a few days of sulking she'd forgiven me. Today was our first day of freedom, and we were still celebrating.

"Well, it's good to see you," Barbara said, and Brent clapped his hands and laughed as if he were happy, too.

"Have you heard anything from Stuart?" Elizabeth asked.

Barbara smiled again. "So far, I've gotten five letters," she told us. "He's still in the hospital, but he's getting better every day."

"Are they going to ship him overseas?" Elizabeth asked.

"They can't," Barbara said. "His father broke his eardrum."

"You mean he's deaf?" Elizabeth stared at Barbara.

"Just in one ear," Barbara said. "But that's enough to keep him out of combat."

"My mother told me the army will court-martial Stuart," Elizabeth said. "She thinks he could be executed or sent to jail."

"No," Barbara said, "nothing that bad will happen, Elizabeth. As soon as he's strong enough, Stu says he'll have a hearing. My dad thinks the army will take a lot of things into consideration—his family, what his father did to him, his attitude toward war."

Barbara paused to remove an acorn from Brent's mouth. "Where did you get that?" she asked him. "Dirty, dirty." Making a face, she threw it away and took a teething ring out of her pocket. "Here, isn't this nice?" she asked as the little boy put it in his mouth and grinned.

Turning back to Elizabeth and me, Barbara said, "If Stu had deserted in Europe, he'd be in serious trouble. Your mother's right—you can be shot for that. But Stu went AWOL before he was sent overseas. The army could put him in jail or give him a dishonorable discharge, but I hope Dad's right and they go easy on him."

"I bet your folks were sore when they found out Stuart deserted," Elizabeth said.

"Dad was a little upset," Barbara said, "but Mother claimed she knew it all along."

Elizabeth whistled, and I knew she was thinking about the hairbrush her mother had used on her rear end when she heard about Stuart and us.

"Sometimes you start to feel the killing just has to stop," Barbara said. "You don't want anyone else to go to war. Especially somebody like Stu."

There was a little silence. I was thinking about Jimmy, and it must have showed in my face because Barbara put her arm around me and gave me a hug. "We'll all miss Jimmy," she whispered. "College Hill won't be the same without him and Butch and Harold."

With the wind tugging gently at our clothes and hair, we walked quietly down the path beside the trolley tracks. The March sun was warm, and the forsythia bloomed like spilled gold in front yards. Elizabeth balanced on the narrow tracks while Brent watched, laughing at her wavering steps and outspread arms. I walked beside Barbara, my head tilted back, looking up at the small white clouds scudding across the sky. They reminded me of a flock of sheep driven home by the wind.

"What about dumbo Gordy?" Elizabeth asked after a while. She teetered for a moment and concentrated on regaining her balance as if she were more interested in walking the rail than hearing the answer to her own question, but she didn't fool me. Even though Elizabeth wouldn't admit it, not even to me, I knew she missed him.

"According to Stu, Gordy's having a great time at his grandmother's house," Barbara said. "Best of all, Mr. Smith's gone out to California, looking for work. Stu doesn't think he'll be back."

We were almost to Garfield Road when Barbara stopped and looked at us. "Can you two keep a secret?" she asked. "You can't tell anyone, not yet. I haven't even told my parents."

Solemnly, Elizabeth and I crossed our hearts and hoped to die if we ever revealed a word of what Barbara was about to say. "Girl Scout's honor," I added for good measure.

"Stu asked me to marry him," Barbara said.

While I stared openmouthed, Elizabeth leapt off the trolley track and hugged Barbara as hard as she could. Turning to me, Elizabeth grabbed my hands, jumped up and down, and whirled me round and round. "I knew it, I knew it," she shouted.

After a few more leaps, Elizabeth let go of me and seized Barbara's arm. "When's the wedding? Is it soon?"

"Not till next winter," Barbara said. "It depends on the war and what the army decides to do with Stu."

"Margaret and I will be your bridesmaids," Elizabeth told Barbara, "and Gordy can be the ring bearer."

"What a wedding that would be!" Barbara threw back her head and laughed. The March sun caught the red in her hair and made it shine.

Then, her face serious, she said, "You only get one wedding like that, kids, and I've already had mine. This time, Stu and I are going to the county courthouse, but I'll make sure you know all about it. If you hadn't dragged me down to the woods last winter, who knows what would've happened to Stu."

We watched Barbara walk away, the wagon bouncing along behind her. Before she disappeared around a corner, Brent looked back at us. "Bye-bye! Bye-bye!" he called. "We go, we go!"

We waved to him and Barbara and then kind of swooned against each other. It was exciting to know we'd been involved in a big romance, even helped it happen.

Elizabeth punched me lightly on the shoulder. "Didn't I tell you she was in love with him?"

I grinned and nodded my head. "You were right as usual," I admitted.

"I always am," Elizabeth said. Running ahead, she shouted, "Step on a crack, break Hitler's back! Step on a crack, break Hitler's back!"

Over our heads, tiny red buds softened the maples' bare

branches. A robin, the first one I'd seen, hopped across Mr. Zimmerman's lawn, and two squirrels darted round and round the trunk of a tree, as if they were playing a game of tag. It was almost spring, and we were beating the Nazis. Soon it would all be over, both in Europe and in Japan. No more bombs, no more bullets, no more killing. Barbara would marry Stuart, and we'd all be happy again.

For a moment I imagined our family riding in that brand-new car, heading toward Ocean City. Daddy driving, Mother reading the map, Jimmy and me in the back seat.

Shocked at myself for forgetting, I stood still, my eyes shut, and forced myself to remember. Jimmy wasn't coming back. Forever and always, there would be just three of us. Mother, Daddy, and me. There might be a car, there might be a trip to Ocean City, but there would be no brother to call me funny names or make me laugh. Never, never, never. My eyes filled with tears, and I stumbled on an uneven place in the sidewalk as I walked slowly down Garfield Road.

Already halfway home, Elizabeth whirled around to look at me. Her hair spilled over her eyes, her pea coat hung open, its last button dangling on a thread, and her overalls had a big hole in one knee. "Come on, slowpoke," she shouted. "Step on a crack!"

It had been a long time since I believed our game would hurt Hitler and bring Jimmy home safely. But, to please Elizabeth, I yelled, "Break Hitler's back!" and stamped the sidewalk hard the way I used to.

Elizabeth watched me run toward her. The wind had

dried my tears, but from the way she grabbed my hand, she must have known I was feeling sad.

For a moment we stared into each other's eyes. Lots of things had changed since the war started, but not us.

Linking my little finger with hers, I smiled at Elizabeth. "Forever and always," I said, "no matter what happens, we'll be best friends."

Together we walked the rest of the way home.